Pride Publishing books by Bailey Bradford

Single Books

Breaking the Devil
Dark Nights and Headlights
Texas and Tarantulas
Belt Buckles and Cowboy Boots
Something Shattered
Yes, Forever
The Jasper Soul

Southwestern Shifters

Rescued
Relentless
Reckless
Rendered
Resilience
Reverence
Revolution
Revenge
Reluctance
Renounced
Retrograde

Southern Spirits

A Subtle Breeze
When the Dead Speak
All of the Voices
Wait Until Dawn
Aftermath
What Remains
Ascension
Whirlwind

Love in Xxchange

Rory's Last Chance
Miles To Go
Bend
What Matters Most

Ex's and O's
A Bit of Me
A Bit of You
In My Arms Tonight
Where There's a Will
My Heart to Keep

Leopard's Spots
Levi
Oscar
Timothy
Isaiah
Gilbert
Esau
Sullivan
Wesley
Nischal
Justice
Sabin
Cliff

Mossy Glenn Ranch
Chaps and Hope
Ropes and Dreams
Saddles and Memories
Fences and Freedom
Riding and Regrets
Broncs and Bullies
Hay and Heartbreak
Vaqueros and Vigilance

Coyote's Call
Off Course
In from the Cold
Blue Moon Rising

Mystic Tattoos
One Too Many

Spotless
Hide
Hunt
Home
Heart

Coyote's Call
Off Course
In from the Cold
Blue Moon Rising

Valen's Pack
Run with the Moon
Exodus

The Vamp for Me
My Life Without Garlic
Don't Stake My Life on It
Sunshine is Overrated
Don't Drink the Holy Water
The Trouble with Mirrors
That's One Cross Vamp

Calendar Men
Mr. January
Mr. February
Mr. March
Mr. April
Mr. May
Mr. June
Mr. July
Mr. August
Mr September
Mr. October
Mr. November
Mr. December
The 13th Month

Power

Exchange

Submit

Dominate

Wild Ones

Destined Prey

Destined Predator

City Shifters

Bearly There

Harey Situation

Fire and Flutter

Dragon Dreams and Fairy Wings

Wyvern Ways and Elven Magic

Intrinsic Values

Artifacts

Antiques

Anthologies

What's his Passion?: Unexpected Places

What's his Passion?: Unexpected Moments

Racing Hearts: The Lonely Ones

Intrinsic Values

ANTIQUES

BAILEY BRADFORD

Antiques
ISBN # 978-1-83943-733-5

Interior text design by Claire Siemaszkiewicz
Pride Publishing

Published in 2021 by Pride Publishing, United Kingdom.

Pride Publishing is an imprint of Totally Entwined Group Limited.

ANTIQUES

Dedication

To everybody who's ever had difficulty in going after what you want.
Never give up.

Author's Note

Artistic license—no pun intended—has been taken with the works of art and galleries mentioned in this story...and much of the police procedure was adapted for story purposes.

Chapter One

Elliot Douglas knew he should have been hurrying. He detested being late for anything, considering it disorganized at best and impolite at worst, when he prided himself on being neither of those things. In addition, he was very much looking forward to this appointment. No—he very much *needed* this appointment. While those undeniable facts made him lengthen his stride a tad, his interest in the architecture and design of the houses on the midtown streets he was walking along meant he kept glimpsing things that grabbed his attention.

As the proprietor and manager of San Antonio's Intrinsic Value antiques shop, his wide-ranging interest in art and design had him taking in everything from the houses' building styles to their colors and trims. He'd been to many well-known interactive museums and ever since his first visit to this area of San Antonio had thought of it as a living architectural gallery.

His whimsical feeling that he should have a chart or worksheet so he could tick off examples of the different building types all around him made him smile. Maybe he should make something along those lines, some mini poster to be labeled and even colored in? *Edwardian, Victorian, Tudor…* His quickening steps echoed the rhythm of his thoughts that listed the design styles he passed. *I would design that, yes, if I could draw.*

Should he have chosen this neighborhood to settle in? The question surged whenever he came here to Tobin Hill, where his love of collectible objects and period pieces had him slowing down to appreciate details of everything from lawn or porch furniture to hanging lanterns or even lampposts that caught his eye. If his pace slackened, it was because of that and nothing to do with him being in his forties. Forty-two wasn't old, no matter how old-fashioned he was or even how he might feel at times, and Elliot kept his six-foot-plus frame fit and in shape.

But the visual appeal of this community, and the location, so convenient for his store, had him second-guessing yet again the area he'd actually bought real estate in. *Well, too bad.* With all the work he was putting into his property, he couldn't see himself moving. And besides, he really liked his house, his refuge from the world.

His destination was in sight, and he hurried up the short drive and onto the small porch of the square ranch-style house, smiling anew as always at the realtor description of these nineteen-seventies stucco properties as "California bungalow style".

There would be no need to lift the brass knocker, so Elliot raked both hands through his light-brown hair to settle the slightly long waves that sprang from his temples, trying not to think that he'd combed his fingers through where his hair had started to silver. He even went to polish his wire-framed glasses before remembering he didn't wear them in the daytime any longer…which of course had him blinking, aware of his relatively new contact lenses.

"Lars." Elliot greeted the man who'd opened the door for him and who now stood back to usher him in with his usual pleasant, welcoming expression.

"Elliot." Lars was discreet, never saying Elliot's—or anyone's name—until the front door was firmly closed. He tended to blend into the room, tasteful yet unremarkable, and was now unobtrusively noting Elliot's arrival on a slim handheld tablet, the dark-gray cover of which he flipped open and immediately flicked closed again.

The computer equipment had grated on Elliot at first. He wasn't at all a fan of technology, but he knew he couldn't expect people to keep track of appointments in ledgers or books these days. And goodness, he had a cellular phone—as he still called it—himself nowadays. A friend from the club where Elliot exercised and swam worked in IT and had helped him choose a sleek, slimline model. Nothing big or bulky or flashy, and Elliot was still in the forgetting it in his office or kitchen phase of coexistence with it.

Karl, the man he was here to see, came out into the waiting room and regarded him. "Good morning, Elliot. Do come on in…or do you need another minute yet to look around and think how you'd decorate and furnish the place?"

He'd told Karl about that silly habit of his, something he did in homes or stores or restaurants, and Karl had found it charming, always remembering it.

Elliot gave a rueful nod of acknowledgment and, casting his eyes down, walked past Karl into the next room, where there was calm and peace and barely audible soft music playing. He waited for Karl to enter behind him, close the door and sit, then nod toward a chair for Elliot to seat himself.

"You walked here?" Karl asked, his steely blue eyes catching the light. The morning sun made his neatly groomed dark hair, short beard and mustache shine. He probably chose to sit where he was on purpose and his stillness ensured he'd remain in the light. "Elliot?"

"Oh, excuse me. Wool-gathering. Yes. I like the walk. It's part of coming here, for me. A warm-up."

He knew what he meant. The distance was nothing from Intrinsic Value, in the city's cultural Pearl District, but more of a stretch from his home in Lavaca.

"And you came from home? I'd hate to think you were at work so early." Karl gave him an assessing once-over. "Help yourself to water." His short, sharp chin jerk indicated the jug and glasses on the small table. "Have you been overworking since your last visit?"

"Well..." Elliot hedged, pouring himself a little water that he didn't want and wouldn't drink.

"Elliot. You know better than that." Karl sharpened his tone a little. "Tell me."

He hadn't gone into recent...*incidents* in any great detail with Karl but had shared some of what had been happening at the store and with his employees lately. Now he caught Karl up on how things had finally settled down again after the events that had been set in motion when Elliot had purchased items from the Buckman sale.

"I swore off them, but I did go to another estate sale last week actually. There's the local art and antiques fair coming up soon and I have a list of items to look out for there," he finished.

"With most of them being for your house, on which you're still working nonstop," Karl surmised. Elliot dropped his gaze. "But you've found time to relax, to exercise? You look in great shape."

Elliot's face heated at the kind words. "Swimming most evenings, and I took up squash again." More like he'd forced himself. But…

"Excellent. And we'll have you switching to racquetball soon!" Karl's eyes gleamed and he stood, motioning Elliot to his feet with a quick crook of his fingers. "It's time. Go on through."

Through into what Elliot thought of as the *real room*, after he'd showered and prepared, of course. Elliot was used to older mirrors, in the store and his house, and tended to avoid modern ones, but the full-length bathroom mirror here didn't give too stark a reflection. The recessed lighting made his eyes seem more tawny than brown when he peered at his irises, checking on his lenses. Towel tucked around his waist, he walked into the treatment room. *The real room.*

"Elliot." Karl coming in the other door caught him by surprise. "You're not lying down."

"Sorry," Elliot muttered.

"Don't be sorry. Be more obedient." Karl took off his suit jacket, leaving him in his shirt and vest. He rolled up his sleeves, revealing his muscular forearms. He was powerfully built, with quiet, contained strength.

It was starting, frissons whispering down Elliot's spine. Nodding, he lay on the table, swallowing at the snick of the door being locked, then the splat of the oil being pumped. The noises, the scents, were familiar, as were Karl's hands smoothing his upper back and shoulders. Him pressing strong thumbs up the nape of Elliot's neck had Elliot holding in a moan.

"Head to the side on the rest...hands on the wings..." Karl ordered, a second before the table's mechanism popped out the armrests either side for Elliot to hold on to. In seconds, a padded strap snaked across his neck, holding his head in position and leather straps were buckled around his wrists, keeping his hands in place.

Buckled by Lars, who Elliot hadn't even heard come in or lock the door again after him, although Elliot knew he would have, just as he knew Lars would now position the flat mirror to the side of the head of the table, angling it in such a way that Elliot could see what Karl would be doing to him. *Everything* Karl would be doing to him.

Karl paused, even after Lars finished, making Elliot shiver and ask, "Now what?"

"You know what." Karl whisked Elliot's towel away, leaving him naked. In seconds, the table's end section was extended and widened, spreading Elliot's legs to Karl's satisfaction, and further straps secured his ankles to the corners. He peeped in the mirror—he was fully bound, as pulling at his bonds showed him.

"The ball gag, I think," Karl said.

Elliot shook his head.

"Hmm. I'll let you have that..." Karl's voiced faded as he appeared to think. A quiet command had Lars offering him a tray from which Karl made his choice of the selection of bandannas it held. He twisted the cotton cloth into a strip and made a knot in its middle, tying another on top of the first to make it bigger. Big enough to gag Elliot, when placed in his mouth and the fabric tied around the back of his head.

"I like the look of over-the-mouth on you," Karl reflected. "And it soaks up the saliva. But it's the ball gag next time."

The hard edge to his voice had tiny tremors rippling Elliot's skin and his rapidly filling balls had him shifting on the table.

"Although I do like to hear you," Karl commented, drawing a sharp fingernail down Elliot's spine.

Elliot, eyes wide, struggled around the gag.

"You struggle so prettily," Karl told him, watching his face.

Elliot didn't think he looked pretty at all. He thought he looked like the thickset, almost middle-aged man he was. But here, at Karl's, he *felt* pretty, perhaps, and loved the sensation. He thrilled at all the different feelings that each part of the appointment provided, and underlying them all was pride in himself for having taken this stride toward what he needed. *Another step out from behind the wall I built around myself.*

Karl's "Ready?" had hardly reached Elliot's ears before Karl delivered the first blow, an open-handed spank to one ass cheek. Although Elliot knew what was coming, the first strike was always a jolt, a blow he felt radiate out from the point of impact to his toes in one direction and his head in the other—Karl hit hard. Elliot breathed out around the cloth in his mouth, riding the sensations in the few seconds Karl allowed before he followed the initial smack with a second to the other cheek, one that made Elliot pant through the gag.

More powerful, meaty smacks followed, Lars' quiet voice counting them. Having Karl's sub witness what his Dom, Karl, did to Elliot was part of the process.

"Ten. And that's the warm-up."

Elliot was almost relieved. He was already burning, tears slipping from his eyes. He turned slightly to catch Lars' impassive expression and that added to the sensations buffeting him. He turned back to see Karl in the mirror, shaking out his hand.

"Now, sting or thud?" Karl watched Elliot's hand and repeated, his voice harsher, "Elliot, sting? Thud?"

On the second choice, Elliot curled his fingers twice, their agreed signal for yes. Everything they practiced was always pre-negotiated.

"Good." Karl took a wooden paddle from the flat box Lars held out to him. He motioned to Lars to loosen Elliot's gag a little. "How many?"

"U…up to you, sir," Elliot managed before Lars replaced the gag again.

"Is the correct answer."

Elliot thought Karl rewarded him for it by hitting extra hard.

"Five, I think…" The blows Karl, pro-Dom, landed were precise. He'd never once come anywhere near to striking Elliot's hip or tailbones. The impact of each tightened every nerve in Elliot's body and fired heat through every vein, intensifying with each hit.

"*Ai'ive,*" Elliot counted, as well as he could around the soaked cloth in his mouth.

"And now the other…" Karl murmured, and selected a new paddle for Elliot's other butt cheek.

"*No!*" Elliot implored through the gag, trying to struggle. "Nuff. Can't take more…"

Karl waited a few seconds then bent low to speak next to Elliot's head. "Oh, you'll take it, Elliot. And any more protest, and I add strokes to the tally."

That extra bite, that element of being forced that inch beyond what he said he could handle—*thought* he could handle—was everything to Elliot. It had started with being strapped down—he still remembered his struggles—then having another person witness his play... All things Elliot had barely understood deep down in the recesses of his psyche that he craved. But he was starting to understand more and more...and act on his needs.

Karl straightened and began again, and there was only the impact, the blows, and Elliot's soul vibrating to each one, to take him soaring. Heat burning through him, he was shaking and sweating when Karl finished. He had his eyes closed, but felt hands undoing his straps, then Karl was helping him to turn over. He cried out when his abused ass made contact with the table.

"Look at you." Karl's voice held admiration for Elliot's straining cock, the head wet and shiny with pre-cum. "How badly do you need to come?"

This was another Karl question that didn't need an answer. "You're going to wait a full minute. Do not touch yourself until I say. Understood? Say the word."

"Understood." It came out in nothing like his usual cultured tone.

The second hand on the large wall clock had never moved so slowly. Elliot, desperate, was just beginning to suspect something was wrong with it or that Karl had rigged it, when Karl nodded. "Do it. Let me see you."

It didn't take Elliot long. A few pulls at himself, a loud moan and he climaxed over his stomach and chest, his body a rigid arch off the table. His eyes on Karl, basking in the warmth on his face and the praise he loosed, Elliot milked his cock to the last drops. He accepted the soft tissues Karl held out to him to dab at himself. It didn't matter, because the session always finished with another shower.

His after-shower always felt totally different from the one before, and now Elliot was less keyed up, he could appreciate the finer details, such as Karl having ready the bergamot and sandalwood soap Elliot liked, which he used at home. Elliot lathered his body, wondering as he always did if he'd ever have someone do that for him, in the same ways as he'd soap that person, both of them caring for the other.

He made himself wait until he was toweling himself dry to examine his ass cheeks. What he saw had him grinning, and not just at the reddened color—the paddles Karl had used on him had been imprinted.

He'd tried to glimpse the words or designs on them during the session but had been unable. Now, though, he stared at his right cheek, with its new image of a heart, right in its center, and at his left, which bore the word *love*. He did love it, every aspect of coming here, the service Karl provided, the careful way he ran his business, how it didn't feel like a transaction…

As much as Elliot thrilled to the anticipation and thrived on the acts themselves, he also loved the winding down. The final stage was always out on the back porch with Karl, for light chat and the herbal tea they both enjoyed…and Elliot forced himself not to wince at how sitting on his recently paddled ass felt.

"Do you get to the club much?" Elliot thought to ask. The place they'd met, where Karl played as a Dom.

"Not as much now." Karl put his cup down. "And I know you don't either. The atmosphere's a little different in there recently. I think there are some changes on the horizon—I heard it's getting a little harder-edged, more extreme, and maybe new management? But we'll see if the changes are for the better. Some can be."

Elliot's preference for a routine was a half-joke between them. When he stood to go, Karl looped a hand around his upper back to bring him close. "Take care," he murmured.

Elliot started his walk to the store. He felt good, lighter, as he always did after a session with Karl, yet heaviness was creeping in sooner than it usually did. He reviewed the progress he'd made. Trying to come out from behind the barricades he'd shuttered himself behind, he'd gone for coffee with a couple of guys from his sports club and even a drink once, but there'd been no spark.

Then, when he'd come to understand that rough, submissive sex was what he craved, he'd gone looking for it in Caress, where there were plenty of Doms. But as much as he might crave to play in public, the idea of subbing to someone he didn't know, who didn't know him, and who Elliot didn't know if he could trust, made him freeze up.

He'd found a good compromise in Karl and his behind-closed-doors service. He liked the kind of man Karl was, and also their arrangement, but couldn't help envying what Karl and Lars had.

What must that be like, that sort of relationship? To be with someone he could give all of himself to, voice all his needs to, and for that person to act on them with him...because they met his needs too? And all of them, including companionship, domesticity... He'd never had that and doubted he ever would.

"Wishes and dreams, maybes and moonbeams." It was a silly expression of his grandmother's, one he hadn't thought of for years, and it came to him out of the blue.

No. Elliot focused on the day ahead, on his schedule, what he'd be doing and when. He planned to order something different for lunch—that was the next brick he was going to topple from the wall around himself. Maybe one day, in the future, he'd be ready to take bigger actions, but for now…

Now was longing, as tenuous and as strong as a moonbeam, slipping through the cracks.

Chapter Two

"Wind your neck in," Detective Sergeant Andrew Harrington advised his fellow DS Claire Arthur as he drove them past the front of the new riverfront court. She was tilting her head so far back to take in the tall apartment buildings that she was almost lying flat.

"So, admit it now?" she asked. "That it's as stunning as they say?"

"*Spectacular.* Just look," Drew mocked, slowing to a stop at the gated entrance to the underground parking garage. "The security has designer uniforms, and I bet there's a better class of dimly lit allocated parking facility, that's for sure."

"Metropolitan Police Service Specialist Organized and Economic Crime Directorate," he announced, presenting his warrant card, his police ID, to the uniformed guards. "Here to question Roman Kislyak." He took pleasure in the surprise on the guards' faces at that. *Good. Let word spread.*

"Interview," Claire, leaning over, corrected Drew. "*Interview* Mr. Kislyak. Specialist Crime Directorate,

Arts and Antiques Division." She added a bland, professional smile to her mitigating words.

One of the uniformed men brought an IT console to life, running Drew's name against the expected visitors programmed in for the day. The other guard smirked at Drew's car. Drew understood. As a detective, he wasn't driving a squad car, but obviously no resident here would be seen in a mid-range saloon like the one he was in.

"You're cleared to enter, officers. Please take these." The guard on the console handed over security lanyards. "These must be visible at all times. Please make your way to space PV2 and wait to be escorted." He opened the gate for them.

Drew and Claire looped the badges' cords over their necks and Drew nodded to show he'd understood the man's instructions then proved he had by driving inside to the designated visitor parking spot for the penthouse and cutting the engine. He reached for the door handle, but Claire put a hand on his before he could ignore what he'd been told and get out.

"You know what I'm going to say," she said.

"Yeah. What Detective Inspector Lassiter wants you to say."

"What our DI wants *us* to say and do. Which is that Kislyak is a renowned art dealer and is *not* a suspect"—she raised her voice over his scoffing noise—"because there's no evidence against him. Fine, you've had him in your sights for a while now, but we have to tread very carefully. Like, tiptoe. Really daintily and delicately. Like ballerinas. On a tightrope. Balancing cut-crystal glassware."

"All right!" Claire could represent her country at the Olympics if talking were an official sport. Drew

suspected Lassiter had paired them up as she filled the silences he tended to leave. "Funny that you're supposed to be 'the brakes to my accelerator', or so Lassiter said when appointing you," Drew mused.

"Funny when I'm the one with the runaway tongue? Yeah. Hilarious. Side-splitting. Rib-tickling. Rolling—"

"You're an excellent detective." He didn't give praise lightly—Claire Arthur was someone he was happy to work with. Just as well, with there being just four detectives in the Specialist Crime Directorate division they worked in. He and Claire were the only sergeants, ranking over the two constables. "And nothing but the best for someone like Kislyak," he finished.

"By that you mean rich and well-connected, right?" Claire inquired, using this minute of down time to check her appearance. She tucked in a few strands of red-brown hair.

And an international criminal hiding in such plain sight that he might as well have been lit up in neon. Drew nodded. Claire nudged him to draw his attention to the staff member approaching their car.

"Let's get to work?" Drew suggested, exiting the vehicle and straightening his tie and suit jacket. He kept his dark hair short on the sides and its slightly longer top wasn't enough to need smoothing down, just as his designer-stubble-length beard was too short and neat to be wayward. Control was key.

The male employee reached them and held up his lanyard to identify himself. "Thames Side Court concierge. You would be the Scotland Yard, erm, personnel?"

The Met was still informally known by its older name, and Drew supposed it sounded less brash than anything with the word *police* in it. "That's correct. Detective Sergeants Drew Harrington and Claire Arthur, here to ask Roman Kislyak questions about a stolen painting he sold." He flashed his toothiest smile, and Claire face-palmed.

"I… Right. Well, I'll walk you over to the private elevator." The guy, not tiptoeing as Claire had mentioned, almost sprinted them along the wall to a row of doors. "And hand you over to…"

It seemed the elevator door that opened for them wasn't the one he was expecting. Drew checked it was one of the small bank for the penthouse. It was, so he didn't see an issue.

"Yes, this one," the man who was waiting in the elevator said.

*Or should that be man*servant, Drew wondered, entering. *Or butler?*

The elevator set off, its action smooth, and within seconds, they'd reached ground level then were climbing aboveground.

Claire let out a gasp. "Oh my God!" She pointed at the glass wall as if Drew weren't aware that they were ascending the building…the outside of the building. They rose above the embankment and the river itself, its bridges and the roofs of the capital's monuments. "See? Enviable river vista and stunning views over London!"

It was breathtaking, but Drew shrugged. "*We're* on the Thames embankment too."

Claire's grimace said that their place of work, farther down the bank of the river, had nothing in common with this shining glass tower, not in location or style. "How the other half live," she breathed.

"More like how do the other half live with themselves?" Drew muttered. How many of the owners of these high-end river-facing Westminster apartments had acquired them by less than honest means?

From his cursory research alone, he suspected the purchase of at least three apartments had been made through money laundering, a means to wash the illegal gains of criminal activities, the cash moved in from overseas. And if he were right about Kislyak, a sizeable part of the Ukrainian's profits came from stolen artworks that were sold on to unscrupulous buyers, mainly in Russia, Saudi Arabia and the UAE.

Not that Drew was accusing the man in question of doing the actual stealing. Drew couldn't imagine the art dealer getting his hands dirty at this stage of his career. Kislyak presented as sophisticated, cultured, attending gala events and contributing to charities and foundations. He was a hard man to get close to, keeping to his elevated circle, although rumors suggested he was also involved in less high-flying…organized crime. Maybe because of that, he was a harder man to even get to see. Drew burned with curiosity to look him in the face after all the research he'd done on him.

Claire sighed, obviously still enjoying the view. "Can we not start until we reach the destination, but enjoy this for a few more seconds?" She shot him a look, reading his face and stance. "Yes, I know. Crime never sleeps."

"Not even in penthouses," Drew agreed, stepping toward the door when a soft, muted buzz announced they'd arrived.

"Oh, I guarantee you won't find any evidence of *any* crime here," said the man who'd ushered them out of the elevator and who followed behind them. The challenge in his voice had Drew twisting around to him. *Man…but no servant. The fucking bastard!*

"Roman Kislyak," the man said with a smirk as big as his penthouse. His voice was smooth yet had a catch to it. Not as tall as Drew's six-foot-something, he was stocky, almost shaven-headed and looked…non-descript, in thick-framed glasses and a featureless black jacket.

A snap of his fingers had a valet easing that garment from him and slipping a more tailored blazer over his linen shirt. Kislyak pulled a chunky gold watch from the blazer's pocket and wrapped that around his wrist, waving the servant away when he moved in to help. He slid the glasses off, taking up a pair of much more stylish tinted aviator sunglasses, and in the few seconds it took him to put them on, Drew saw that Kislyak's eyes were so dark brown, they seemed black. The man they'd come to interview now stood tall, looking down his nose at Drew.

He laughed, glancing at Claire. "I'm glad you approve of my home."

Claire's cheeks reddened. "It's amazing, sir."

"And this is only the hallway." Kislyak gestured. "Let me show you the wraparound terrace and the three-sixty-degree views of London you've no doubt heard about." He looked from her to Drew. "I suppose I should apologize for catching you out. I can never resist that trick."

"Could be risky." Drew didn't move or blink his blue-gray eyes. "You might hear something you don't like."

"Or that I wasn't meant to." Kislyak didn't move either, and Claire shifted, preparing to speak, but

Kislyak's upraised hand stopped her. He held out his other hand to Drew, who had no choice but to shake it.

"Detective—" Drew started.

"Sergeant Andrew Harrington," Kislyak finished for him. "I know. Or, let's say I made it my business to know...who's investigating me."

So, someone he'd been questioning about Kislyak had blabbed to him. That was only to be expected, when money this big was involved. Kislyak strode ahead, and they followed, out onto the terrace he'd mentioned. It was as wide as a café esplanade but much more lavish, with modern sculptures on plinths and even a fountain.

"Sit." Kislyak dropped into what was probably a priceless chair and pushed more out with his feet for them, the noise jarring. "Enjoy the famous vistas."

On the surface, it could seem a polite invitation, and the broad smile accompanying it an example of the charm the man was known to employ, but the hairs at Drew's nape stood up in reaction to Kislyak, and he bet Claire had a gut feeling about him too. *That he's a crook.*

Drew had strong feelings about liars and cheats—the higher up the food chain they were and the more untouchable they felt, the more he burned to bring them down. He'd seen enough to despise those with power who used it to take advantage of or, worse, threaten and coerce, those weaker than them. And not just in the course of his police work, but in the events that had propelled him into law enforcement, when his father had taken the fall for company embezzlement that he'd had nothing to do with.

Leo Harrington had been bewildered at his inability to prove his innocence and anguished to finally understand that his manager had not only been working with the head of accounts to cover their tracks but had left a trail that pointed at Leo as the accountant responsible. Leo had been the one blamed for endorsing and cashing customer checks payable to the company, then keeping the funds. Leo was the fraudster who'd set up a bank account with a fictitious name similar to the company's to divert electronic payments into.

His father's horror at being found guilty of a crime he hadn't committed had stuck with Drew, as had the smooth lies told by people whom his father had assumed were friends but who'd lived and operated in deceit and double-dealing.

Drew looked around at the terrace, the view, the small clump of hovering servants…all signs of Kislyak's wealth. "Art dealing pays well," he remarked.

"I make it so." Their host flashed a smile and snapped his fingers, which had his staff scurrying forward. "I'm about to eat. Won't you join me?"

Drew wanted to roll his eyes at the almost cinema-villain act. He shook his head and Claire refused too, although her gaze was glued to the salvers being uncovered as the staff served Kislyak brunch. A maid poured glasses of iced water and fresh orange juice for all three of them. He wondered if Kislyak would say Grace before he ate. If he did, it would likely be the art dealer's version—*For those we are about to deceive, may the Lord make us truly grateful.*

"You have questions for me." Their host didn't look up from the poached egg he slit with his knife, to make the yolk run down its side.

"Your father, Viktor, after he made money when state utilities were privatized, started by acquiring authentic, but not well-known, works by artists such as

Gauguin, Chagall, Modigliani and Klee." Drew ignored Claire's start of surprise at his question. He took out his notebook, although he didn't need to refer to it.

"That's not a question." Kislyak still didn't look up, instead spooning salt onto his egg.

"No, background," Drew agreed. "He was in business with Anton Selaman and was involved in what came to be called the Curious Case of the Twin Chagalls."

Kislyak's fingers tightened around his knife, but his gaze was on his plate.

"Because it seemed their business model was to copy these little-known works then sell the reproductions in Asia and the originals in Europe and the States, hoping that original and copy would never meet. It worked fine as a system...until it didn't, with two identical Chagalls up for auction in two different houses at the same time."

Now Kislyak looked up, his eyebrows one low, straight, menacing line. "That was Selaman."

"He was convicted of the fraud, yes," Drew agreed. He flipped over a page. "Then your father, and you to some extent, switched tactics to 'filling the gaps' in artists' bodies of work, either inventing new works or creating ones which were believed to be lost but whose titles were known...no images of which existed."

Kislyak slammed his knife and fork down. "That was my father's assistant. He was deceiving us."

The man had pleaded guilty and died in prison, but Drew doubted he'd been working alone. "And now we come to you." Drew gave him a smile. "You and stolen paintings." Because he was convinced that Kislyak had switched tack again, to a different form of art fraud.

Kislyak took up his phone and his thumbs flew over the keypad.

"What my colleague means is we're inquiring into the Van Gogh painting *Saint-Rémy-de-Provence Orchard* that Sonia Malykhin, wife of Mikhail Malykhin, received as part of her divorce settlement and sold at auction," Claire said, the polite cop to his rude one.

"Or tried to, but couldn't, because the painting in question was stolen goods." Drew laced his tone with concern. "You sold Malykhin the artwork, yes? And yes, that's a question."

"I did. A lamentable incident. I bought it in good faith in Zurich from an elderly couple who had had it in their family for many years. They kept no paperwork, but I had the work authenticated by three experts in different countries and submitted their reports with the work." Kislyak's answer came out pat. *Rehearsed.*

"Oh, the painting's real…just stolen goods. From a robbery at the Hauser Foundation in Zurich in 2015…at the same time as you were in that city," Drew snapped. He was sorry to spring this on his partner—she had no idea that Kislyak had been in Zurich when the small foundation had been robbed. Not many people did.

Kislyak swept his arm across the table, knocking his plate and glasses and their contents to the floor. "Bland and undercooked," he shouted at his staff, who scurried to clean it up.

"Two other Van Goghs were stolen at the same time, the entire short series *Saint-Rémy-de-Provence Lovers at Twilight* and *Saint-Rémy-de-Provence Church at Sunrise.* Did you also acquire those?" Drew stared at his quarry. "You sell mostly in Russia, Saudi Arabia and the UAE, places where buyers don't really care about provenance or if certificates of authenticity are fake..."

Kislyak smirked but said nothing, and Drew saw red. His phone beeped, as did Claire's, but he ignored them. He stood. "Roman Kislyak, I'm arresting you on suspicion of—"

"Wait!" Claire held out her phone, showing him the screen, where the name of the sender, Chief Inspector John Caine, was clear, as was his message. "We have to leave right away, sir," she told Kislyak.

He texted him! He fucking texted Caine and Unable who's put the brakes on this! "No," Drew began.

"What a pity. I'll show you out." Kislyak shoved his chair back and stood. "I'll even give you a short tour, seeing as you like the place so much." He strode off, leaving them to follow.

"Not here," Claire gritted out before Drew could speak. "Let's get outside."

But that took time, with Kislyak leading them through a couple of rooms, pointing out the place's features and décor. Claire nodded and made all the right noises, and Drew stared narrow-eyed at a wall of paintings and took out his phone, still ignoring his boss's message.

"He's guilty, Claire," he said as soon as they were back in the car. "You feel it too, don't you?"

"Doesn't matter what we feel, when we've been told how to handle him and we ignored an order," Claire replied.

"It doesn't matter that he was laughing in our faces? Or that he's a criminal? I know he is and I'll prove it."

"Better do it quick then, because we're in deep doo-doo." Claire started the engine with a jerk and peeled out of the parking space with a squeal of rubber. "Deep shit, even. Right up to our necks."

Drew let her drive, because he wanted to study his phone, more specifically the photos he'd discreetly taken in the penthouse, of the artworks on that one wall. Kislyak's tastes were expensive, flashy and brash, so why did he have a row of softer, more Romantic maritime, landscape and seascape paintings? They didn't fit the room or his style.

It nagged at him and when things did that, he wanted to understand why. "I'll prove it," he muttered, firming his lips.

Claire sighed. "But don't you have a date tonight? You and your fella?" she asked.

"Do I?" Drew didn't remember. Any plans he and Ash had would have to be shelved. Bringing down that evil bastard was more important.

Chapter Three

"Gooooal!" cried the spectators, and Elliot, despite knowing nothing of five-a-side, understood that a team had scored, and, as it was the team that he was here at Olmos Basin Park this evening to support, that this was a good thing.

"Yes! Well done!" he called through the wire cage onto the field. *No – the pitch.* Darrell and Aldric had gently corrected him again as to that terminology when he'd arrived, at the interval. *No – half-time. Look at me, becoming quite the expert.*

Or, at least, he'd be more familiar with the game and the league if he didn't tend to tune out when Aldric Beamer, his employee at Intrinsic Value, talked about it. In Elliot's defense, that had been quite a lot. Aldric had been enthusiastic right from his partner Darrell Williams' initial idea of forming a five-a-side soccer ball team, mainly of other police officers from the San Antonio Police Department, to participate in OutField, San Antonio's largest LGBTQ sports association.

Darrell enjoyed sport and fitness, and Jonas, the other employee at the store, had joked that this was Officer Williams' latest scheme to get Aldric to take more exercise and improve his diet. Remembering that silly joke had Elliot smiling now, holding his hand over his mouth in case anyone saw and thought he was amused at the standard of play he was watching. Elliot supposed he was lucky that Aldric and Darrell hadn't been badgering him more to join in.

"It's for everyone!" Aldric had blinked his big brown eyes behind his glasses. *"From beginners like me who can barely kick to fantastic athletes like Darrell, and if you're male or female, or gay or straight! Oh, or transgender."*

And it's a social event as much as a sports activity, Elliot surmised, sharing a nod with a fellow spectator. The crowd had been chanting and singing, and even dancing and doing something Elliot had learned earlier was called a Mexican Wave. People were drinking beer and hadn't Aldric mentioned something about a get-together, after? The atmosphere was festive already.

A photographer left the fenced-off area and turned to face the crowd, raising his camera to perhaps get a few shots of the huddle of men in furry bear masks behind Elliot. Elliot scooted away, out of camera range.

"Elliot? Elliot Douglas? Is that you?" asked a voice at the side of him and although it was familiar, when he turned to see, it took him a moment to place the client he'd begun working for recently, an interior designer looking for items for the spaces he created for commercial and private clients. The man had been dressed more formally on the couple of occasions they'd met, and his thick blond hair had been tidily slicked back.

"Hello. Lovely to see you, James." Elliot put out a hand to shake, and James gave him a quizzical look then pulled him in for a brief hug, delivering a quick slap to Elliot's upper arm with it.

"Call me Jim," he replied. "James makes me feel I'm at work."

"Ah. So I shouldn't ask you how things are going at the apartment building?" Elliot was interested in how the former cannery was becoming a residential development, and particularly in the loft James Devlin Designs and Interiors was creating. "And how the glassware looks?"

"A half-wall studded with pale-green glass items of the nineteen-thirties." Jim nodded, his eyes misty. "It's coming on well. I'll take any and all Depression glassware you can find me! Oh, and do you remember me mentioning the neighboring apartment, that they were interested in my services too?"

Elliot nodded, wondering if this would impact on the store. He was always happy to consult with decorators and designers and find pieces for their projects.

"Well, they were, and we're already underway, and they've gone for a classic look—the nineteen-eighties!" Jim's enthusiasm bubbled from him. "You remember, all black, gray and red tones, diagonal and geometric patterns? So moody!"

"And pictures of Ferraris and Porsches on the walls?" Elliot vaguely remembered. It wasn't a style he was interested in.

"And I found a cache of original airbrushed posters, all bright pinks and blues, from an old shop in the area—I swear they have every sort of print known to man."

"Out in New Braunfels?" Elliot knew it. Well, the art and antiques world here was small. Everyone in it knew everyone else.

"And that's enough shop talk, agreed?" Jim cast a look around the spectators and over the pitch. "Is this your sort of thing?" When Elliot didn't reply immediately, he rephrased. "Who are you here for?"

"Oh, I'm supporting my employee and his partner who play for—let me get it correct—Here's The Kicker. They're in the lead." He might not have been into team sports or the finer points of this modified version of soccer, but he could read names and numbers on a scoreboard.

"I see." Jim clapped and cheered at the final whistle. "Well, I hooked up with a guy who plays with the Bexar Bears and so I thought I'd hang around." He gave a subtle tilt of his chin to where the Kicker's opponents were lining up against the fence to receive applause from their supporters. "The big…bear Bear. You never know…" He waggled his eyebrows as if in mockery, but there was genuine hope in there, Elliot felt. Jim waved and left.

Elliot had been right that the match was followed by a social event. The players reappeared, now showered and changed, making Elliot think *he* should have changed into less proper attire before coming to the game. Jim had looked a little surprised to see Elliot dressed as if to greet clients, but he didn't really possess a wide range of casual clothes. He had sportswear, for playing squash and for swimming, and rough, workman-type clothes for when he labored on his house, but any other pastimes he indulged in tended to call for formalwear.

Music started, and people drifted onto the now-open pitch and some headed up into the nearest row of seats ranging around the field. A jingle of bells and the blast of a horn sounded, people cheered and food and drink carts trundled up.

"You found *healthy* hotdogs?" Aldric was asking Darrell incredulously when Elliot joined them.

"*Artisan* hotdogs," his partner corrected. "And an organic juice cart, look." He pushed a lock of Aldric's brown hair, fluffier than ever with being wet and drying, back from his eyes. "Don't tell me you only wanted to join the league for the snacks after each game."

"Not much chance of that when you're in charge of organizing the food and drink." Aldric attempted a pout, but couldn't keep it up, especially when Darrell swatted his ass. He grinned at Elliot. "I mentioned the after-game was as big a part of it as the game, didn't I?"

"You did, and I see that you were correct." Elliot was thirsty and wanted to peruse the soft drink options, but found his attention drawn to Aldric, who was glowing with more than the aftermath of exercise.

It was astonishing how much the painfully shy, socially anxious young man had blossomed in such a short time. Aldric stood almost jigging on the spot to the lively music playing from the speakers. He was smiling and chatting, and with a couple of players from the other team. He presumably didn't know them as well as he did his own teammates, but that didn't stop his face lighting up and his voice almost singing as he described the handmade ice-cream wagon someone had booked for last week's game...and that had sold beer-flavored ice cream. He basked in the attention, the exclamations and questions that greeted his story.

As much as Elliot would have liked to take credit for Aldric's newfound confidence and spirit in that he'd spotted his potential and given him a job at Intrinsic Value—*given him a chance in life*—he couldn't. Aldric having fallen in love with Darrell, and being loved in return, was responsible. Elliot was very happy for him, glad he'd found his special someone. Neither of the couple had had an easy time of things so far in life—both having, well, *uneven* relationships with their families, was a polite way of putting it.

Elliot could relate to that. He pulled his thoughts away from that direction. "*You find your life family, once you make your own life,*" a wise man had told him. He'd been a detective, so maybe being around Darrell, a police officer, had brought him to Elliot's mind. The case Elliot had brought to him had furthered his career, and Elliot was glad about that, too.

Life family, he mused. Yes, he'd gone some way toward finding that. A more usual expression with the word *life* was life partner, and that…*no*. He didn't see that on the horizon.

"Oh, I haven't congratulated you! How remiss of me. Well played, Kickers. You all did an excellent job." Elliot reminded himself to sound less formal. "How many goals did you score, Darrell?"

"Two. Aldric set both of them up. We make a good team." Darrell threw Aldric a warm smile, making him blush.

"Anyone want to join the line for dogs?" Aldric asked.

"Yeah. I promised myself the gourmet, with hoisin, garlic and ginger sauce. And there's fries with Parmesan and rosemary. Sound good, Elliot?" Darrell asked.

"I'm hardly a culinary expert. I tend to have the same meal over and over, but, yes, it sounds interesting," Elliot replied. "I believe it's a big game next week?" Aldric had mentioned it. "And that Aldric's brothers are coming to watch?"

"And Darrell's brother Ryan with his fiancée Leah," Aldric half-turned to add, speaking over his shoulder where he was studying the menu. "Maybe he'll convince his other brother, Travis, to come along too."

"Is something the matter, Aldric?" Elliot narrowed his eyes to study him. The boy was fizzing with excitement.

"We have…well, not news." Aldric glanced at his partner. "Well, it is something new. To us, I mean. Two things. Nothing big, but…"

He barely held it in until, carrying their food and drinks, they stood around a small table. "You tell him!" he demanded of Darrell.

"Aldric co-signed the apartment lease." Darrell ruffled Aldric's hair and fed him a fry. "Finally."

He'd moved in a month or so back, but this made it official. "Congratulations." Elliot picked up his plastic cup of herbal tea in toast.

"And Darrell won't let me pay half the rent," Aldric said, chewing and swallowing his mouthful of meat and bun.

"Because…" Darrell drew it out like a drumroll. "He's decided to go to college!"

"Just community college, locally," Aldric added.

"Excellent! I'm very pleased to hear it. Have you chosen which?" Elliot nodded as Aldric described the merits of San Antonio's biggest community college over the others in in the city, and all the subjects he hoped to study during the course of his associate degree. Aldric really was making his own life.

"Ask Jonas for advice?" Elliot suggested. "I realize he teaches at a different sort of college, and on bachelor's degree courses, but even so?"

"Over here!" Darrell called, and signaled before Aldric could reply to that. He waited until the man he was waving at joined them. "Elliot, you asked how many goals I scored? The other side of the coin is how many goals the Bears *didn't* score, because Nando stopped at least six dead certs."

Darrell's green-brown eyes were alight with intent as he half-pushed the newcomer into the middle of the group—next to Elliot. "Nando plays in goal," Darrell added, demonstrating understanding of Elliot's unfamiliarity with the game. "He works at the same station as me—Officer Nando Reyes, Elliot Douglas, Aldric's boss."

"Pleased to meet you." Curly-haired, short and tan, Officer Reyes was softly spoken and looked a little diffident, although the grip of his hand was almost as strong as Darrell's.

Elliot caught the look that Darrell and Aldric exchanged, and his heart thudded. Reticent and reserved, he'd never discussed his sexuality with them, but it seemed clear that they were if not setting him up with their friend, then getting them together in the hope that something would come of it. Why did they think he was gay? He was, but that wasn't the point. Before he could think what to say, the guy spoke.

"Do you play?" the police officer asked, stumbling over his words. "Five-a-side, or kickball or baseball? You should join one of the teams."

"I wouldn't have a clue, I'm afraid," Elliot, trying his best not to take the irritation he was feeling out on this innocent party. "The closest I get to a team sport is attending an arts and antiques fair. They can be rather a scrum. I feel I have to get into training for the one coming up next week." And yes, he was sounding stiff and out of touch again. Well, if he was behind the times, at least he knew where he was.

"I think we need another box of fries." Aldric elbowed Darrell. "Anyone want anything while we're there?"

Elliot shook his head, and Nando refused too. Elliot hated to see the other two walk away. It left him exposed and vulnerable.

"Do you play pool?" Nando asked, still trying.

"I used to play billiards."

The word brought back memories of the game and when he'd played and with whom, memories he'd rather tamp down. He regretted his reply for another reason when Nando continued, his voice eager, "There's a bar downtown with a billiards table."

Elliot swallowed his sigh. He willed Darrell and Aldric back so he could make his escape. He might want someone of his own, but this sweet, shy man, a little reminiscent of Aldric when he'd first come to work at the store, wasn't the one for him. He wouldn't be able to meet Elliot's needs any more than Elliot would be able to give *him* what he wanted.

He felt lonelier now than he had before he'd forced himself to come here.

Chapter Four

Claire looked up when Drew slid the takeout coffee and sandwich across her desk. "What's this?" she said.

"I got them. Make up for you missing lunch."

"Drew, it's almost *evening*!" Claire exclaimed.

"Is it? Oh." He'd been working all afternoon, and, seemingly, into the evening. "Keep them until tomorrow?"

He pushed them nearer as a peace offering anyway. How things had gone with Kislyak had been his fault—he'd railroaded his fellow detective sergeant into it and had made sure their superiors, especially Detective Inspector Stewart Lassiter, their immediate boss, knew it. It hadn't stopped Lassiter passing on the shit he'd received from Chief Inspector Caine, of course.

"Yeah?" Claire picked up the sandwich. "Then this better be *at least* chicken Caesar and bacon. And no runny egg. I saw enough of that earlier."

"It is. And I know. Oh, and the coffee's got a shot of caramel in, how you like it." Drew leaned lower. "Look, I'm sorry. I know I'm a little—"

"Obsessed?" Claire flicked the lid of her drink and sniffed it. "Just the one shot, I see, or rather smell?"

"But I know he's connected!" Drew raked his fingers over his scalp. "Not just planning out these huge, lucrative thefts, but the whole of Organized Crime would *love* to know the source of his 'unexplained wealth', all the properties and business he owns in the UK, bought through anonymous companies and—"

"DS Harrington!"

Drew straightened, closing his eyes. The exasperated voice behind him belonged to DI Lassiter.

"You got any real info on the role of offshore companies and trusts washing money leaving Russia or the Ukraine, take it to the Criminal Finance or the Financial Investigation departments!" his boss barked. "If not, I suggest you sit your ass down in your chair and get on with your job."

"Sir."

Drew sat his rear down as ordered and pulled up the Art Loss Register and Interpol's Stolen Works of Art database. It was part of his job to send updated information to the registries on any new losses reported or pieces recovered, and he enjoyed being the bureau's Interpol liaison. He studied the lists too, cross-tracking thefts over the last decade with what he knew of Kislyak's movements.

The Zurich robbery had been dominating his thoughts ever since the painting stolen from there had come to light. Tracing the chain of ownership from Sonia Malykhin to her ex-husband had led to the dealer the Russian had bought it from, then to how Kislyak had 'acquired' it.

Drew pulled off his black-framed glasses and held them in the hand he was using to prop up his chin as he considered all he knew…and what he suspected. A more typical kind of art theft was low-key, surreptitious, taking advantage of the lack of funds available for strong security to steal from museum storage facilities or library stacks, for example. The scant resources these places had often meant it was years before thefts were discovered, also making the dates of the crimes impossible to pin down to anything more concrete than 'sometime between this inventory and the last one'.

But robbing a gallery, and in the various bold, brash ways several had been raided? That was a whole different kettle of crime. *Brash, arrogant…*adjectives he'd use to describe that egotistical bastard Kislyak. Was he the type of criminal to direct robberies of foundations and institutions like the Hauser?

"Lucky?" he called across to Detective Constable Kai Lee, who had no objection to his nickname, though he probably would if he knew the song and singer it referenced, Drew bet. "You got that info on the 2019 case?"

"Just printing…" At the copier, Lucky gathered up several sheets of paper into a file to present to Drew. He'd send it all in e-form too, and log it into their workflow, but Drew preferred having actual pictures to look at, even if they were only copies, like these, while he committed them to memory.

"These all of them?" Drew asked.

"From the 2019 robbery at the Maison d'Art Moderne, Paris? Yes," Lucky assured him, hovering in case he was needed further.

"Thanks." Dismissing him, Drew fanned the pieces of paper out like playing cards. Monet's *Fishermen at Île de Groix,* Renoir's *Bather Seated on the Grass,* Cezanne's

Sunrise at Châteaufort and Sisley's *Wheat Field Near Ponthierry* along with another Monet, one of his *London Bridge* series. The priceless works of art had been on loan from several museums for an exhibition, netting the raid a good haul.

Was Roman Kislyak in Paris at the same time? A phone call requesting that information from the official departments privy to the knowledge could alert the system—and his bosses—what he was checking into, but Drew had other resources. He picked up the phone.

"Chris, hi," he greeted his contact. "I was wondering if you could—?"

"Lemme guess. Look up your nemesis in the archives again," Chris interrupted, his eyeroll coming across the phone line perfectly.

"He's hardly that," Drew scoffed. Okay, so he was a little fixated on the guy. *A little.*

"Can I remind you again that *London Society* magazine, while the city's oldest illustrated journal of society, doesn't have a high-powered database like the sort you have at your disposal?" Chris sniped. "All we have are issues on file. I can't cross-reference by search terms."

"I know, and all I want to know is if Roman Kislyak shows up in Paris in June 2019."

"Oh." Denied anything to bitch about, Chris hummed and muttered as he looked it up.

"Anything?" Drew waved off Hasina Ali, the department's other detective constable, who was trying to draw his attention to a memo she'd left on his desk.

"Any*one*. As in, anyone who was anyone was in the City of Light then for a huge international charity fashion show and gala dinner at the Paris Opera House. Ooh la la."

"Roman Kislyak included?"

"Roman Kislyak included."

It proved nothing, of course, especially with the man attending and donating to a lot of high-roller charity events, but it was a connection.

"You stalking him?" Chris inquired. "Because if so and because I'm an enabler, I can tell you where'll he be this evening. We're covering it."

Drew had to grin. "I'm not." Fine, so his bosses might disagree. "But tell me anyway?"

Chris did, and Drew hung up, then turned back to a photograph of his quarry. He could believe the man was cunning and motivated enough to plan heists, but, now he'd met him, he couldn't see the man sitting calmly, analyzing and directing others.

No, Kislyak wasn't as much a person who saw an opportunity and took it as someone who *made* an opportunity and *grabbed* it, neutralizing anyone or anything in his way. All that aggressive, explosive energy that swirled around the man needed an outlet.

Drew's fingers brushed the memo Hasina had just left him. Glancing at it had him clenching his teeth. The department's short-term focus was now on looted antiquities, which were an economic opportunity for terrorists who found them, sold them and used the funds to finance further operations. "For God's sake!" he gritted out. "Yes, this is vital, but the Met has other units for this!"

"Don't blame me. I'm only the messenger," Hasina called.

"Did you read the supporting documents that informed the new directive?" Claire asked him. She took some stapled sheets of paper from her desk and brought them to him. "Basically the same info as we got from the presentation the other day about looted cultural property being terrorists' second-highest source of income. Oh, and the high international demand for ancient artifacts and the relatively low risk of selling them compared to drugs or weapons, yadda yadda..."

Drew knew all that. "What if I can prove Kislyak's into organized crime?" he said, because all the trails he was investigating—as far as he could get along them—led to that. These lines of inquiry tended to fall apart, though, with any would-be informant clamming up and muttering that it would be the kiss of death to spill anything on this.

Claire reared back. "Is there any point me repeating what our DI and our Chief Inspector said? Well, all I can say is if you take a shot at the king, you'd better not miss, you know? For your sake."

Shaking her head, she left him. Drew grabbed his phone and again studied the photos he'd taken at the Thames penthouse. A search told him the three paintings were a James Buttersworth ship portrait, a Martin Johnson Heade seascape and a Bricher landscape. The ship was rendered in great detail, and the other paintings more Romantic, the artists from different schools. Different periods even. The only immediate link Drew could think of was that all three were from the US and still popular there.

His phone buzzed as he held it and he took a brief glance at the text. Ash, his boyfriend, was at Drew's flat, cooking. *Fine.*

"You going?" Claire pulled her coat on. "Big evening, right?"

"I'm going in a minute." Drew nodded. He didn't know if the evening would be big, but he hoped it would be fruitful…

* * * *

Should I be doing this? He wasn't dressed for it and didn't have a ticket for whatever was happening at the Lakeside Gallery, Kensington Gardens, but the memory of Kislyak's smug *I'm untouchable* smirk propelled him on, and his badge got him through the security rope around the gallery's pavilion. He wouldn't be crass and help himself to a drink, though. There wasn't a show on—this was a private event. A drinks party, Chris had said, some preliminary view of the early stages of an exhibition being held soon, for some of its sponsors and consultants.

A small flat-screen on a display plinth told him what was being put together, and his cop senses tingled. *A Celebration of The Impressionists* was going to bring together artworks from around the world, including some rarely seen, from five decades of the art movement. Images of the works flashed up—all the big names, and the places they were coming from were major, from huge museums to private collections.

Drew studied the building where this show would be held. He did a circuit of its outside, noting its size, strengths and weaknesses. It was small and without half the security measures a major museum or gallery had. How closely this fitted the pattern of the two heists he was investigating staggered him. Small like the Zurich foundation, and about to be stuffed full of extra priceless works on loan.

It has to be! He increased his pace to return to the doors, where an information panel stood. He had to know when this was opening, when the works would be arriving. *The Met has to know.*

As he neared the door, a man strode out by the side of a woman, a small group of people following. Dressed in well-cut evening wear, he held a glass of wine high and gestured with it as he described something. *Kislyak.* He saw Drew, and his face hardened into a dark scowl. He strode over, that coiled-spring energy Drew had noticed wound tighter.

"What the hell are you doing here?" he snapped.

"My job." Drew stood still, making the other man fidget. "Which is, as you know, looking into burglary of art and antiques, international cultural property theft, fraud and money laundering."

"You're not needed here." Kislyak's face cracked into a fake smile. "Not when I've already got one cop on hand…" He swung aside so Drew could see the small huddle of people who'd exited the gallery behind him. "John?" he called, sounding stressed and upset.

John being Chief Inspector John Caine. *Of fucking course.*

"I invited him and his wife as a thank-you for John's apologies for one of his men *badgering me.*" Kislyak's voice rose on the last two words—they were aimed at Caine, who rushed up, spilling his wine, his face like thunder.

"Sir—"

Caine held up a hand. "You are not required to speak. You are not required to be here. So leave, now, and this will be dealt with as soon as possible. Expect to face disciplinary action." He turned to Kislyak.

"With all due respect—" Drew started.

"Go home!" Caine ordered, loudly enough that people looked over. "Or I'll arrest you myself!"

Drew carried the image of Kislyak's gloating sneer with him all the way back to his apartment in Putney. He slammed the door behind him.

"Ash!" he called to his boyfriend, remembering he'd said he'd be there. "You won't believe what…" The flat's general darkness struck him, that and the candles burning on the small kitchen table where Ash sat, a plate of untouched food in front of him. A similar plate waited opposite him, and a bottle of wine and glasses competed for space in the middle with a vase of flowers. The flat smelled of more complex cooking than the pasta or rice dishes Drew or Ash usually threw together.

Drew walked into the kitchen, which was Ash's cue to blow out the candles on either side of his plate and stand to snap on the harsh overhead light.

"I'm late," Drew began.

"About half a year late," Ash agreed. He took a few cooking utensils from the cupboard and shoved them into a bag. "As in, tonight was our six-month anniversary…" He indicated the table.

Shit.

"Six months of missed dinners, canceled evenings and postponed dates. I know you're busy. So am I." Ash Patel was a mergers and acquisitions lawyer in the City. "But this was the final chance, to see if we were going anywhere, and we're not. Well, no—I am."

He zipped the bag closed. "I think I've got everything I might have left here, but if I missed anything, bring it to my office and leave it at reception. Don't bother trying to get in touch with me." He scoffed. "Why am I bothering to say that? You won't. Too busy obsessing."

"Ash," Drew said, his voice low and deep.

"And don't use your Dom voice on me. Yes, sex is good between us. *Really* good. You're focused on me and my pleasure, and we're compatible there. But a relationship is more than that, even a Dom-sub one." Ash shook his head. "You'd think I'd have seen the signs, six months back." He slapped door keys onto the table and blew out the last candle.

"Isn't that a little dramatic?" Drew asked.

Ash grabbed his bag and left, without replying or saying goodbye. As the door closed, Drew's phone buzzed. He pulled it out and read the message from Caine. It had him sinking onto a chair, almost dropping his cell. *Really?* He hadn't been expecting this, although perhaps he should have been.

He looked up, his mind whirling as he regrouped, made new plans. At least now he had the freedom to go after his obsession.

Chapter Five

"I understand," Elliot assured his employee. Aldric had been so excited to come to his first fair, his first trade event, for all it was a local one, in San Antonio's revitalized Southtown area. He'd been talking about it all last week and even studying the list of items Elliot would be keeping an eye open for, hoping to spot treasures.

The boy had been keen to be involved and help, but was finding the building's size, the number of stalls it held and the amount of people buzzing around them overwhelming. If Aldric thought this was oversized, Elliot wondered what he would make of the city's Rose Palace.

"The event center is bigger than places you usually frequent, yes?" he asked his assistant, trying to soothe him. He nodded to a fellow trader he knew.

"And fuller and louder," Aldric had his eyes half-closed.

Yes, Elliot couldn't really see the still rather shy young man in packed clubs, where the press of bodies against his was part of the appeal. "But we're here nice and early, before it gets too crowded," he informed Aldric.

"Really?" Aldric, his face screwed up, had his hands raised, as if he were thinking of covering his ears. His action pulled his shirt collar away from his neck, revealing a large hickey, evidence of the young couple's active sex life...and the slight SM tinge to it that Elliot couldn't help noticing in Aldric and Darrell's interactions.

"It's going to get busier?" Aldric repeated.

"Really." Elliot had to smile. "Aldric, why don't you go back to the store? I know we closed for the day, due to the fair, but should you prefer it, I'd be happy for you to return to Intrinsic Value and either open for business or catch up on stock taking or cleaning. I'll be fine."

"I...think I might." Aldric nibbled on his bottom lip. "If you're really sure?"

"I'm positive. I have the list of pieces I hope to find, for the shop or clients." *Or the house.* "I'll avoid impulse buys, after the last one." And yet the train of events that had followed Elliot's snap purchase of a box of curios from a sale hadn't been all bad—Aldric had met Officer Darrell Williams as a result.

"And don't feel you have to stay working late, to make up for your late arrival," he ordered his over-conscientious employee.

He waved Aldric off and considered how best to make his way around the stalls. The former warehouse complex had been made into a big hall and smaller side rooms, the plan being to turn it into a congress venue. Its huge loading and docking bays meant there was plenty of parking, and Elliot hoped the blight that had tainted the area was gone. He caught sight of Jim Devlin and waved. Jim came over to greet him.

"I always feel like I'm on a day off at these events," Jim said. "Especially when I'm looking for kitsch."

"Oh, the apartment you mentioned?" Elliot raised his voice to be heard over an announcement.

"No, I'm fitting out a nightspot. I can't say which…but I will say if you find yourself at a bar on The Strip that has a huge glitterball, think of me." He winked. "Oh, talking of, I joined Caress! It's a club…a BDSM club."

"I know it," Elliot replied. *I'm a member.*

"It's been open a while but undergoing some changes, I think." Jim nodded. "New management, I understand. Should freshen it up. I'd better dash. Catch you in a few, no doubt."

Jim's talk of Caress made Elliot wonder if he should pay it a visit. He hadn't been in a while and, if nothing else, he should check his membership was in order, if the club was under a new owner. Pondering this at the back of his mind, Elliot made his slow way from stall to stall, vendor to vendor, greeting people he knew, checking off the goods on sale against his wish list.

A stall over to one side, hugging the wall, caught his attention, or, more specially, the art it held did. The luminist landscape depicted in one painting gleamed, serene and calm, its stretch of water a soft blue and its sky a gentle haze. It looked like a Bricher.

Elliot's habit of mentally rearranging or redesigning his surrounding kicked in and he thought that he would never have displayed that tranquil scene next to a painting of a ship, rendered in meticulous detail. The painting on the other side of the graceful clipper had him frowning, running the muted colors of its salt marsh landscape against landscape artists he was familiar with. *Oh, of course.*

"It's a Heade?" he asked the stall holder. "And is the clipper ship an actual Buttersworth?"

The luminist was a Bricher, according to the signature. Elliot had lost himself in art right from when he'd been a small boy, staring at pictures in the family encyclopedias, and these American artists took him back to childhood. As a child, even the artists' names had fascinated him, especially the longer or foreign ones, and he'd learned them all.

He knew these three, all of them having three names— Martin Johnson Heade, Alfred Thompson Bricher and James Edward Buttersworth, though they were considered old-fashioned now. Elliot's more business-orientated family had never understood his absorption, then had thrown him a sop by giving him an expense account to decorate his own office as he pleased as soon as he'd joined the family firm.

"Sorry? I didn't catch your reply, I'm afraid," he said to the seller.

Probably because the man hadn't given much of one. Dealers didn't tend to be chatty, but they usually managed more than grunts. The guy wasn't local. "You have some lovely pieces," Elliot went on, although he considered the three paintings by the famous American artists the best things on the stall. "Where do you normally sell?"

"Corpus Christie," the man answered.

"Oh, do you usually sell to the Traylor Art Gallery?" It was a good place to buy original paintings, both from well-known, acclaimed artists and emerging talents.

"Yeah." The dealer looked past him.

Elliot's stubbornness kicked in. "Do you have a card I could take?" he inquired, taking his own silver card case from his pocket and sliding one free. "Here's mine, and I do hope you'll give my store a call when you have new acquisitions."

The man made no move to take it or hand Elliot his own card. "Gave my last one just now," he said.

Already? Well, that's poor organization not to have sufficient supply. Elliot studied the man's stall as a whole. The rest of the paintings were nothing special but were of similar maritime or seascape natures. The three that had caught his eye could be genuine—the works could have come from a house clearance, for instance. *But buyer beware.* "I'll be back," he promised the seller, who didn't seem as if he cared either way.

Elliot turned toward a stall bearing Victoriana. He knew the seller, and she'd called him about a matched set of free-standing column oil lamps it would be possible to convert to electricity—Elliot wasn't that much of a purist—and had mentioned a box of period fireplace tiles, too. Focused on that, he didn't take in the beeping noise or the commotion behind him at first, but shouts and screams had him swinging around to see what was wrong.

Even when he saw, it took him a few seconds to make sense of what was happening. A small group of men, all similarly dressed in nondescript dark clothes and black masks, were snatching and grabbing goods on the stalls nearest to the emergency exit, yelling at the stallholders and bystanders not to resist or stop them or come near.

A raid! Elliot hurried to take cover behind another stand. The men must have smashed their way in through the emergency door and were sweeping up the contents of the stalls either side of it, shoving what they could into sacks. Elliot had no sooner thought that than the gang backed away, making for the door again to escape. It had taken a minute at most, yet seemed to last longer, with Elliot, along with most people there, he imagined, standing frozen, holding his breath.

He was wrong. Not all the gang had run for the exit. One was struggling with a vendor. The majority of the sellers hadn't resisted, had obeyed the yelled instructions, all except one, the man with the paintings Elliot had just been looking at. Now, shouting and screaming, he clutched one this thief was trying to make off with, leaning over his stall to yank it back while the robber tried to pull it free, like a sick game of tug-of-war.

There came a sudden glint of metal, the black-clad raider lunged forward, and the stallholder fell back, clutching his chest, out of which a metal spike now stuck. Not a spike, a knife, with blood gushing from the wound. Elliot's hand flew to his mouth and his legs carried him forward—he had to help.

"No! Stay back!" people around him shouted, but he was the nearest to the victim. The assailant was gone by the time Elliot reached the stall—the denuded stall, the entire row of paintings having been swept into the big sack the thief carried. The man he'd been speaking to minutes earlier wouldn't care. He was slumped back into the wooden chair he'd been sitting on when Elliot had seen him, his hands around the knife in his chest…for a few seconds, until they fell limp to his sides.

Elliot stared aghast, barely registering the hubbub around him, the venue staff springing into action, security and medical personnel taking over, the bystanders who'd been nearby shunted into a room at the side of the main hall, all of them exclaiming and recounting what they'd seen or thought they'd seen.

"It all happened so quickly," Elliot said for the second or third time. He hardly knew what he was saying and to whom, until a uniformed officer led him outside to the short corridor the side rooms gave out onto. It was screened-off with a rope at either end and had pairs of plastic seats every few yards, creating makeshift interview stations where other people were speaking to SAPD officers. Elliot sat as directed at the top one just before the rope.

"Elliot...Douglas..." The SAPD officer made sure he spelled it correctly, as well as Elliot's contact details. "You were the last person to speak to the victim," he continued.

"No, that would be the raider. The..." He almost said *murderer*. Because if the art vendor hadn't quite been killed in front of Elliot's eyes, Elliot was sure the man must have died soon after paramedics took him from the scene. The incident didn't seem real. "The person who robbed his stall and stabbed him. They were fighting, the vendor trying to protect his goods. His paintings."

Movement just beyond the rope at the top of the corridor caught Elliot's eye and he looked over, thinking for a second the man was Karl...and stayed looking, because the man was so strikingly handsome it made Elliot's breath catch in his chest. He was about the same height and muscular build as Karl and had the dark hair and almost beard—whatever they called that style these days. He also gave off the sense of stillness and centered power that Karl emanated...and that made Elliot, no matter how hard he wanted to drink in the sight of the guy, drop his gaze. This man's eyes were gray-blue and looked as though they could sparkle with amusement or gleam with intent. The stranger was a top, no doubt about that, and imagining being topped by him had Elliot's ass clenching.

It was probably wishful thinking, but he thought he felt the man's gaze on him as he gave more answers to questions, his mind not really on it, but still thinking about the stranger. He accepted the officer's card and a couple of leaflets informing him about what help he could get after what he'd witnessed. Finished and cleared to go, Elliot was let through the cordon and started to leave.

"Elliot Douglas?"

He froze at his name and knew before he turned that he'd see the intense-eyed stranger behind him. Again, that sense of power radiating from him made Elliot want to lower his eyes but he fought to meet the man's gaze. "Yes? How do you know my name?" he asked.

The man gave a tiny smile. "I heard the officer interviewing you ask it. Are you okay? You must be a little shaken by what you witnessed."

"Are you the...?" Elliot had to think to get the correct term. "Trauma counsellor they spoke about? But you're English!"

"I am, yes. So I can offer you a cup of tea with two sugars," the man joked.

Elliot had been right in his initial assumption—the man could and did lighten with humor. It all made Elliot more confused. "I... Could I see some ID?"

"Oh, I'm not SAPD."

Strange. Elliot would have said he was with the police. "Are you in the trade?" he asked.

"You could say that. And I'd like to talk to you more." Before Elliot could reply that the man, with his air of authority and command had said he *wasn't* with the police, he spoke again, his voice low and deep. "I mean, I'd like to meet you later."

"What?" *He's hitting on me? No.* Elliot must have misunderstood. "Where?" he asked, to put his wild fancy to bed.

This time the man's smile was there, front and center, reaching his eyes. "Judy's. Under the Metropolitan Hotel. I heard it's an interesting place. See you there for a martini this evening."

He walked away, leaving Elliot gawking at his firm ass, his thoughts skittering. *Wait. Did that just happen? That sexy man asked me out on a date…tonight? And he didn't exactly ask, more like expect me to be there?*

Elliot was taking tiny steps out from behind the wall he'd built between himself and the world, but this man, whose name Elliot didn't even know, had just swiped off a whole row of bricks. Elliot couldn't just go out with him like that, could he? *Because if I do, what more will he force me into?*

The shiver that ran down Elliot's back at the thought of that was equal parts trepidation…and yearning.

Chapter Six

Drew walked down the short flight of steps leading to Judy's Martini Bar and cast his eye over the patrons inside, those sitting around the tables and up at the bar that ran almost the length of one wall. The thud of disappointment he got when there was no sign of Elliot told him how much he'd been hoping to see him.

You don't know anything about the guy. That being the case, he had no idea if Elliot would take Drew up on his invite. Maybe this place, with its stylish nineteen-forties vibe, would bring him here, if nothing else?

Had asking him here been the wisest move? *Probably not.* He'd wanted to talk to him—needed to—but the way Elliot had reacted and behaved had intrigued and attracted Drew. That and the man's looks, his slightly long, thick mane of brown hair, starting to silver, springing back from a high forehead, and his tawny-brown eyes. He'd been thinking about him since...and checking up on him too. Everything about Elliot Douglas had captured Drew's attention.

Well, if he didn't show, there'd be plenty Drew could occupy himself with in this place…including the couple of staff who were catching his eye, signaling that there were vacant stools in their sections of the long bar. Drew walked farther along to a spot with a few unoccupied seats next to one another and took one. If Elliot did show, they'd have a little privacy. The bartender gestured, indicating that he'd be with Drew in one minute. Drew took out his phone, thinking to do a little more checking up, when a presence at his side had him turning his head.

Elliot stood there, as handsome and as formally dressed as he had been at the fair and looking just as reserved. It made Drew itch to strip away his layers—literally and figuratively. Drew stood, and gestured to the stool next to his for Elliot to sit. "I'm glad you came," he said, meaning it.

"I…" Elliot hesitated, and Drew knew whatever he said wouldn't be what he'd been thinking, making Drew burn to know his true thoughts. "Had no way to contact you and say I wasn't."

"True."

"And I don't know your name." Elliot settled himself on the stool, looking as though he wished it were a more traditional chair, with a back and armrests.

"Andrew Harrington. Drew to my friends." He leaned in and held out his hand. Elliot's was soft but his grip more athletic than might be expected. No—he was in good shape. His well-cut suit and vest showed that.

"Drew." Elliot tried out the name. "I'm Elliot Douglas. Well, you know that."

"You were thinking of not coming?"

"I…don't get to this area, north of downtown much."

To the gayborhood. Drew liked the careful answer. Again, it felt like a challenge. Not that Elliot was playing coy, or hard to get—more that Drew would have to put the work in. That he shouldn't be doing this crossed his mind again. He had more than enough going on at the moment and no time for distractions. *Tough.* For this man he thought he'd make time. His co-workers would be amazed, as would Ash, who would also be furious.

"Well, this bar caters to all sorts." He lowered his voice. "So are you salty or sweet?"

"E-excuse me?" Elliot spluttered.

"Spicy or sour?" Taking pity on him, Drew indicated the signs behind the bar that boasted of the range of martinis Judy's offered. "Or there's 'strong' too."

"They all seem strong to me," Elliot commented, watching a barman pour hefty measures from two bottles of spirits, one in each hand, into a shaker.

"If I may..." Their bartender popped up in front of them. "I'm Shayne and I'll be your server tonight." He poured small glasses of water for them with one hand and was holding small leather-bound books in the other. "In my experience, you seem sweet." He winked as he handed Elliot the menu. "And you, sir, are spicy." He went to pass Drew a menu, but Drew's arched eyebrow stopped him. "Hmm. Sour, perhaps?"

"I probably *would* like a sweet one, but..." Elliot flicked through the too many pages holding too much information.

Drew leaned close, near enough to detect the sandalwood and floral of Elliot's cologne. The scent was sweet yet had a backbone, a bite to it, and Drew's cock twitched in response. A glance down at Elliot's lap showed he was stiffening, too.

Elliot didn't draw away but stilled, his eyes on the handwritten names and descriptions, although Drew doubted he was taking anything in about s'mores-flavored or strawberry-shortcake martinis. He wanted to get his hand to Elliot's chin and turn his face so Elliot looked into his and read the desire in them, but stopped himself. Elliot wasn't quite ready for that. "Nothing that takes your fancy?"

"It's all a little new to me." Elliot raised his eyes from the page. "I must confess I'm a creature of tradition. Of habit. I tend to stick with what I know." He shrugged, as if in apology for being boring.

Drew didn't find him boring. *More like arousing.* He'd rarely had such an instant and strong reaction to anyone. "Would you like me to let you in on the secret to being in a new place and having to face choices in it?"

"Yes." Elliot's eyes gleamed a rich tawny shade that captivated Drew. He stared into them and watched the pupils dilate. Elliot dry-swallowed, and Drew jerked his chin at Elliot's glass of water.

Elliot took it and sipped, his Adam's apple bobbing. *Fuck,* he was sexy, especially because he kept it low-key, almost concealed. "So, the secret." Drew crooked a finger, and Elliot moved automatically nearer. "Go with the house choice. In this case, the drinks of the day."

"That's it?" Elliot took a second to process, then a tiny smile had his well-shaped lips curving. Christ, but Drew wanted to see them stretched around his cock. "So the sweet martini of the night is…"

"A lemon drop." Shayne already had the lemon vodka in one hand. "And today's spicy is the serrano chili pepper margarita martini."

Drew thought it sounded revolting. "Seems I'm sour. So, a dirtytini, please."

Drew's dirty martini, a mixture of top-shelf vodka and olive brine with real olives, complemented Elliot's choice, something Drew took as a good omen. The drinks were served in large, dangerously close to overflowing glasses, and Drew handed over a bill, telling Shayne to keep the change. The size of the tip told the bartender Drew would rather be left alone until he signaled otherwise.

"So, cheers." He tapped his glass to Elliot's, and they both drank. "The bar has a forties' gangster film feel, doesn't it?" he commented. "Movie, I mean."

"Oh, I speak British," Elliot replied, his wit amusing Drew. "My great-grandfather was from England, and my grandfather was English until the end."

"So you sound like him?" Drew swirled his martini and took another hit. "You don't have quite the same accent as everyone else here."

"No, I'm not a Military City native." Elliot took another sip. "What about you? What brings you here?"

He had to admire Elliot's deflection. "Business…and pleasure."

Elliot dropped his gaze and that natural submission had Drew's balls tightening to the point of pain. He had a gut feeling Elliot was on the same page as him, and Drew usually played his hunches. He did now, doing what he'd wanted to earlier in reaching out to take Elliot's chin to raise his face to his. "Elliot. We could sit here, have another excellent martini, or I could tell you right now how strongly I'm attracted to you and how much I would love to spend the night with you."

Keeping his hold gentle, with no force in it, he nevertheless didn't let Elliot shy away. "I'm staying here at the hotel." Elliot must know there was a hotel above the bar. Drew stroked Elliot's lower face as he let him go. "I feel we have compatible tastes, don't you? You don't have to speak. A nod is fine."

Elliot's full focus on Drew, he nodded, then a complex look crossed his face. "I don't usually do…things like this. This…"

"Isn't your first time?" Drew tried to get a read on him, to help him.

"No." Elliot's voice took on a scoffing note, making Drew raise an eyebrow at his bratty tendencies. "I mean, this sort of thing. This kind of…situation."

"But you want to." Drew made it a statement and received a nod in reply. Maybe Elliot had been in a long-term relationship and was now getting back in the game? Or was shy? Or needed…direction? And damn if that didn't have Drew's cock straining. "Then I'll tell you what's going to happen. I'm going to finish my drink, then get up. If you would like to explore what's between us, do the same."

He swallowed the rest of his dirtytini and stood. His hunches were usually good…and so was this one—Elliot drained the rest of his lemon drink and got to his feet, casting a quick glance at Drew then looking down. How naturally submissive he was had Drew's mouth drying, and he took a quick swallow of water.

"That way." Drew indicated the door, and Elliot set off. Shayne winked. Elliot walked ahead of Drew into the hotel lobby and to its short bank of elevators. Close behind him, Drew pressed against his back when he stretched out to call one. He loved the way Elliot kept his eyes averted on the ride up and during the walk along Drew's corridor.

Inside his room, he couldn't wait a minute longer, pausing only to switch on a lamp before using his body to crowd Elliot against the closed door and take his mouth with a hunger that surprised him as much as Elliot's perfect acceptance of it, the way his mouth opened for Drew's tongue to claim it. The kiss turned into dominance, Drew's arms around Elliot, him mashing their bodies together to feel evidence of his eagerness and his hands sliding down Elliot's back to grasp his ass.

It would have finished with Drew sucking and nipping Elliot's bottom lip—if Elliot hadn't bitten back, and harder than Drew had bitten him.

"You little…brat!" Drew touched a finger to his lip to see if it was bleeding. He didn't think so. He stared down at Elliot. "You know you're getting punished for that, right?"

Elliot's downcast eyes and obedient nod didn't fool him now. Not when Drew caught the glint in those tawny eyes, one that matched the gleam he felt must be beaming in his own. "So, what are you waiting for? Strip."

Elliot stared huge-eyed at him for long seconds before his hands went to his buttons. Each item of clothing Elliot removed and folded, to place in a neat pile, revealing more of his muscular body, had Drew harder and his cock, thick and erect, raring to go. But there were safeguards…

"Nipple play?" Elliot's head-shake was a no. "Hm. I take it bondage is a yes-yes?" Elliot nodded. "And penetrative sex—with condoms, obviously?" Elliot nodded again. That was more than enough for one night. "What are your safewords?"

"Go, slow and stop."

Drew nodded. The man had said he stuck with tradition. "And if you can't speak?"

"If I…?"

"If my cock's so far down your throat when I'm fucking your face that you can't speak, yes. Well?"

Elliot's hesitation told Drew of his lack of practice with that. *Interesting.* "One knock or thump for slow and two for stop."

Drew appraised the man in front of him, his scrutiny bringing a flush to Elliot's face. Drew cupped one side of it. "I'm going to make your other cheeks red too," he warned and loved the catch in Elliot's breathing and the jump his cock gave. The head gleamed with pre-cum, and Drew wanted a taste, but not now. "Depending on how well you handle that, I might fuck you." Oh, he was definitely planning on it.

He undid his tie and pulled it free. Elliot followed every movement, especially when Drew used it to tie Elliot's wrists in front of him.

"I bet you could come right here and now, couldn't you." Drew's low, deep tone was conversational. "With the state of this…" He gave a hard tug to Elliot's leaking shaft. "And these." He cupped his sac. "Tight and already drawn up." He squeezed, enjoying Elliot's gasp and shudder. "And you will, after. There's no spanking bench here, but this chair should do."

He had Elliot walk in front of him again, this time able to admire the flex of his muscles, and kneel in the deep, tall armchair, his bound hands hanging down over its back. He checked Elliot would be able to thud on it easily, then stepped away to angle the lamp for his viewing experience.

"Great ass. Can't wait to fuck it." Drew meant it—his dick was almost poking through his dress pants. He circled so Elliot could see him remove his suit jacket and roll up his sleeves, then resumed his place.

Elliot's rear view was a sight worth seeing, from the top down. His head bowed over the chair showed his neck, and the muscles of his upper back and shoulders were elongated by his arms being bound. His toned back slid into decently sized hips and a muscular ass that had attracted and held Drew's attention. "You swim," he surmised, looking at which muscle groups were more hewn. *And those arms…* "And play… tennis?"

"Squash."

Drew took a second to imagine Elliot in white shorts and tight T-shirt, then in a Speedo. He scratched the fingernails of one hand up Elliot's spine to spear his hand into Elliot's hair and hold his head still. Elliot was a sub who liked to top from the bottom. Drew bent over him to speak into his ear.

"You've been spoiled. Indulged. Petted. Cosseted. No nipple play? Not used to giving head? What a little princess." He tsked. "When I'd love to put you in clamps and those lips of yours would look fantastic stretched around my cock… We'll have to see about that."

He wouldn't, of course, not without negotiation, even if they were practicing consensual non-consent, and he believed Elliot knew that. But the mere words, the idea, sent a ripple of gooseflesh down Elliot's skin, and trilled a frisson down Drew's spine, too.

He gave no warning, just brought his free hand down on Elliot's ass cheek.

Chapter Seven

As much as Drew loved using the flogger on a sub, nothing compared to the skin-to-skin intimacy of a bare-handed spanking—the feel, the sight and the sound Elliot made at the first blow. Drew wished he'd recorded it and could keep it forever. The mixture of surprise, shock and satisfaction went straight to Drew's dick, and he had to take a brief pause. He rubbed the skin he'd heated then began smacking Elliot again, tightening his hold on his head.

Elliot taking a spanking was a sight to listen to—his breaths almost hiccupping out of him as Drew landed each swat—and see, the way his body rose and fell with the blows. By the sixth smack, Elliot was gasping and by the tenth moaning, his cheeks turning from pink to red. Again, Drew wished he were recording this. There was always something special about a first time with a new play partner, and a sub as responsive as this...

He dropped his hand from Elliot's hair to grasp the opposite butt cheek to the one he was smacking, enjoying the broken little groan his sensitive playmate gave in response. Drew realized that the way Elliot had shifted in the chair, pressing into the back of it, was him trying to get enough pressure to his cock to jack off.

"Oh no. No coming until I say…*if* I say," he ordered. "Understood?"

"Sir," panted Elliot, and the natural, unforced way he'd acknowledged Drew's status, his mastery over him and his pleasure, had Drew's heart skipping a beat. It made Drew reward his sub with a very hard swat, one designed to force the air from his lungs in a cry that curled around Drew.

"Like that?" he asked, squeezing then kneading Elliot's reddened ass. He didn't need Elliot's nod telling him that he had. "You're doing so well."

So well that Drew wasn't going to last much longer. "Making me crazy to be inside you," he remarked, as if it were no big deal, just like the way he released one of Elliot's cheeks, admiring the white dimples his fingers had left, then used the forefinger of that hand to stroke down Elliot's cleft and circle his hole. Elliot tried to muffle his cry into the back of the chair, but Drew caught it…and relished it.

Being exposed like that had Elliot clenching, tightening his pucker. "Can't have that," Drew told him, rubbing his thumb over it. "I like a snug fit, but let's get you relaxed." Elliot loosened for him. "You take it regularly. Are you seeing someone? Got a partner?" He should have asked.

"Yes, first and no second," Elliot replied, his breath still broken.

Drew couldn't imagine this man getting it on with a variety of hook-ups, or paying a sex worker, so that was an area to be explored. "Much like this one," he muttered, leaving Elliot briefly to rifle in a drawer and take out supplies. He was desperate to tunnel into his ass, but thought he could stand to play a little first, so tipped some lube onto his fingers and stroked them down Elliot's crease before rubbing them over his pucker, spreading the thick liquid.

Elliot pressing back into Drew's hands earned him a hard slap. "You'll take what you're given," Drew told him, holding the tip of his forefinger at Elliot's hole for long, long seconds before pushing in, making sure to keep Elliot steady with his other hand as he did so. Elliot had the perfect amount of give and resistance, as if designed for Drew's preferences.

God, the man was hot, in all senses of the word, tempting Drew to sink his cock deep into him without preamble. He twisted his finger inside Elliot's channel, pushing until he couldn't go any farther then fucking him one-fingered, loving how Elliot tried to stifle the little moans he gave at each thrust.

"Like that, do you?" No wonder Elliot wasn't into nipple play—he was all about the ass. Drew brought another finger into things, stroking the snug hole, then delivered a trio of spanks to Elliot's cheek. The suddenness made Elliot clench around Drew's finger in reaction…which was when Drew pushed a second into him, working against the increased resistance. This time his groan was louder than Elliot's.

Drew worked his hands in unison, one landing swats and the other twisting and curving, brushing Elliot's prostate. The noises Elliot was making were words now, with *please* and *more* and *yes* prominent in the stream of babble…and making Drew insert a third finger. Elliot had him on fire, his clothes too tight and hot for his body and yet at the same time about to slide off him with the sweat, or so it felt. His arm and leg muscles were quivering and his balls painful. He had to be inside Elliot, even if that meant sliding free of the pull of his ass to wipe his hands on a towel and undo his own belt and buttons, his relief as his cock sprang free immense.

He snatched up a condom and tore it open. "Eyes front!" he ordered when Elliot turned his head over his shoulder, obviously trying to see the reason for the delay. "Yes, I'm going to fuck you. Don't worry about that." He gloved up and slicked up, wondering how badly Elliot was leaking compared to him—he was releasing enough pre-cum that, if he were fucking Elliot raw, he doubted he'd need lube. He lined his cock up to the ring of muscles he'd worked loose and eased the head in, this time letting Elliot push back onto him, although he knew the sub got away with far too much.

He loved that first time taking of a new partner, thrusting his cockhead in then surging deep. Elliot didn't just ripple around him—he *gripped* him, his walls sucking Drew in deeper and deeper until Drew's hips slapped against the sweaty reddened skin of Elliot's ass. *Jesus.* He pulled back, mindful of his partner's discomfort, although the keening noise Elliot was making in response to Drew taking him spoke more of pleasure than pain.

Drew eased out, slowly, loving the sight of his cock emerging from Elliot and the feel of Elliot's channel protesting his withdrawal by pulsing around his dick. He left the bulge of his cockhead just inside, not wanting Elliot to start closing up, then drove his hips forward again, and the sensations this set off in him almost had his knees buckling under him. Pleasure almost too intense to bear slammed into him, so of course he did it again, just to check he could stand it, pulling out and ramming back in, each time taking longer on the out-stroke and plowing harder on the in.

The noise Elliot was making under him, his body rocked by the force of Drew fucking him, was a long, continuous whimper. Drew understood—he was almost whining himself. "You need to come?" he panted into Elliot's ear, and the sharp nod Elliot gave in response almost hit him. He reached around to fist Elliot's dick, the amount of pre-cum making it difficult to grip. Elliot's cock was fat and a decent length, making Drew wonder if he ever topped. Maybe that thought was the added spur that had electricity surging from his balls to engulf his body. God, he wished he'd undressed.

He thrust his cock in hard and fast, working Elliot's dick in time with his strokes. Elliot's entire body stiffened and he shouted, his sphincter muscles clamping down like a vise around Drew. The heat inside Elliot seared Drew, then liquid heat spilled onto Drew's hand, shooting from Elliot's dick. Elliot spasmed, his cock emitting pulse after pulse, wringing him out.

The base of Drew's spine burned, and he gave one last ram of his pelvis, wanting to be buried as deep as he could inside the punishingly tight clutch of Elliot's ass when his climax tore from him, releasing jet after jet of cum into the condom. And still Elliot clenched around him, prolonging Drew's orgasm and squeezing the breath from his body.

He couldn't remember ever having come like this, so hard that his vision whited out and his ears rang, making him hold on tight to Elliot's hips. With difficulty, he stopped himself sagging over Elliot and with even greater difficulty, eased free of his body, keeping hold of the base of the condom as he did so. He tied it off, his arms threatening to shake, and threw it into the trash, then moved to the front of the chair to release Elliot from his bonds.

Being free didn't seem to register with Elliot at first—he remained in position, his head down against the top of the armchair. Drew got behind him again and taking a second to strip off his shirt, rubbed Elliot's upper back and arms, gradually easing him from his kneeling position to get his feet on the floor. But when Elliot went to turn, to fold into the chair, Drew helped him over to the bed to lie down. He fetched a hand towel and cleaned him off, rolling him over to wipe his ass for him too, then stepped over to the minibar for water.

"Here." He started to help Elliot sit, but Elliot managed by himself, finger-combing his hair into place as he did so. He looked far removed from the carefully put together man of earlier.

"Thank you," he said, accepting the water and drinking half of it.

"Thank *you*." Drew felt overheated and overdressed. He toed off his shoes and socks but left his pants on. He chugged most of a bottle of water too and sat on the edge of the bed. "That was incredible. I've never felt such a connection to someone I've just met." Elliot didn't reply so he went on, "It's fine—don't feel you have to return the compliment. Say what's on your mind. What are you thinking?"

"If I can think after that," Elliot burst out, making Drew grin. He could get addicted to this man's wit and candidness. "Are...are you in town for long?"

Shit. It all came tumbling back to him like a rockfall down a mountainside. As unbelievable as it was, he'd all but forgotten his mission in the heat and pleasure of sex with this man.

"Sorry. I didn't mean to force anything, or pry or..." Elliot was clearly misinterpreting Drew's silence. "I just thought you would hardly have come from England for a small arts and antiques fair like today's, that you must be here buying for clients back home, or meetings with people here, or something."

Or something. "I would like to see you again, if that's what you mean," Drew said.

"I'm sorry. Pressuring you, I... It wasn't my intention." Elliot shrank into himself a little.

"You're not."

Before Drew could say more, Elliot heaved in a big breath. "Could we meet again while you're in town? To...to hook up?"

The way he said it, Drew could see this wasn't his normal behavior. That Elliot was doing something out of character by seeing Drew again thrilled him. Then guilt sank through him like a stone. Elliot was perfect for what Drew needed. *Even more so now.* He steeled himself.

"Remember I said I wanted to talk to you?" Drew began. "I still do. It's about what happened today. Earlier. At the exhibition hall."

"The raid? The attack?" Elliot's tawny eyes widened. "You said you weren't police."

"I said I wasn't San Antonio PD, and I'm not." Drew stood. He fetched his ID from his wallet and showed it. "Specialist Crime Directorate, Arts and Antiques Division."

"Scotland Yard?"

He would call it that, Drew supposed, growing up hearing tales of England from his grandfather. He nodded.

"But I..."

"No, of course not. I'm not here for you."

Elliot held up a hand. "Whatever you're going to say, I'd rather be dressed for it, if I may, Officer?"

That stung. "Of course. But you used my name earlier." *And sir.* He still felt the strum of that spontaneously used title on his skin. Elliot going cold on him like this chilled Drew to the marrow.

"That was before I understood you were here under false pretenses. I don't like lies."

Then you're gonna hate this. But Drew had no choice. "I didn't lie. Not exactly. I was at the fair on business. I was interested in the maritime painting and the landscapes and seascapes on the stall that was raided."

"All of them or just the Buttersworth, Heade and Bricher?"

Fuck, he was sharp. And almost as sexy dressed as naked, making Drew lose his concentration. *Weird.* That never happened. "That's a fair question," he agreed. "Because I saw them hanging on the wall of a very wealthy dealer who I believe orchestrates art theft. And that's just one part of what I believe to be the thug's international business empire, which I suspect is far from legitimate. He's impossible to interview, even to get a meeting with, so I have to take a different investigative approach."

"I don't recall paintings by those artists being listed as stolen."

"I don't think they were, until today," Drew agreed.

Elliot was pacing. "I don't understand!" he exclaimed.

"Neither do I." He wished he did, that he knew why Kislyak had shipped the paintings to the States, and had them sent to San Antonio and, specifically to the fair. Drew also wished he knew if the robbery was part of that, or an unrelated coincidence. And he really wished he knew how Elliot would react to what he was going to say next.

"And I *need* to understand," Drew continued. "I need to solve this and soon, because I think I know his next intended target, back in London, and it's in two weeks." When the exhibition opened, although Kislyak could steal from it any time during the month it was being held for, or after, as it was closing, of course. "So I need to be able to move around the arts and antiques scene here, get talking to people, find out information, without arousing any suspicions."

Elliot bending over to see to his shoes make Drew lose the thread of what he was saying. He pulled himself together. "I need help—need a way in."

"And you think that's me." Elliot tied a shoelace with a hard jerk. "What makes you think I'd agree to anything like that?" *To be used like that,* he didn't say, but Drew caught the subtext. Or sub text, he supposed, if they were talking about serving…a Dom.

Drew really hated to do this. "Because I know who you are, Elliot Douglas…or should I say John Douglas Elliot. You didn't change your name much, did you?"

Chapter Eight

John Douglas Elliot. The name thudded into him, hitting him harder than Drew's physical blows had. He'd just about pulled himself together after their session, when he needed to process what he'd just done, how big a stride out of his safety zone he'd taken—how amazing a connection he'd had with a stranger—and now this?

His knees felt a little weak and he reached out to hold on to a chair, glad it wasn't the padded armchair he'd been in earlier, but a simpler office-type chair at the small desk. "Officer Harrington—"

"Detective Sergeant Harrington, if we're using titles. But you've had no trouble with Drew so far," Drew interrupted.

Elliot didn't appreciate the levity or the tiny hint of a smile on Drew's face. Not just then. "I don't know what you might have heard or think you know, but I'd wager it's incorrect." Pulling his formal, slightly old-fashioned persona as tight as he could, he straightened, intending to leave.

"That your birth name was John Douglas Elliot, and you were born into money and privilege and went as expected into the law firm your grandfather set up and that your father and uncle continued and that they…changed the scope of its work a little, shall we say. That is, until you blew the whistle on them for helping clients engage in illegal or fraudulent activity." Drew tilted his head in a *your move* gesture.

Now Elliot did sit, dropping heavily into the chair then wincing. He couldn't believe he'd forgotten that Drew had spanked him and screwed him.

"Hey!" Sounding concerned, Drew bustled away, soon returning. "Here. Drink this." He held out another bottle of water from the minibar, the cap loosened. Elliot took it. "I wish I *could* make you a cup of tea with two sugars," Drew continued, harking back to what he'd said yesterday. "But I can order from room service. I think you—we—should eat something. Is an omelet okay?"

"I'd prefer scrambled eggs." It was true, but Elliot had no intention of being here long enough to eat with this man. If anything, he'd slip out when the room attendant came.

Muttering something that sounded like *knew you were a brat*, Drew ordered on the phone. He replaced the receiver and turned back. "Elliot, I'm sorry. I didn't know saying what I did would affect you like that."

"Really?" Elliot finished his sip of water and looked up at Drew. "I don't quite believe that. Or maybe it's simply that I don't know how people routinely behave when they're being blackmailed."

"The *fuck*?" Drew pulled out the small stool tucked under the desk and sat. Again his reaction seemed genuine, but Elliot, a trader and dealer, wasn't buying anything this man had to sell. "*Blackmail?* Where did that come from?"

"I don't mean for money. As in, I do as you say, or my past comes to light." Elliot put the plastic bottle down and went to stand, but Drew's narrow-eyed stare and low tone prevented him.

"That's not my intention, and I think you know that," he growled.

Do I? Elliot took a good look at Drew, trying to assess the kind of man he was. *Handsome* sprang stupidly to mind, *sexy* following it, and *commanding* on the heels of the first two. None of those helped Elliot right now, when the foundations of the new life he'd built for himself threatened to crumble under him. "What *was* your intention?" he asked.

"You're very invested in playing fair and obeying the spirit of the law. You believe in justice," Drew replied.

"And you got all that from me ratting out my family. Amazing." Elliot didn't recall having been so sarcastic in years. He felt younger, almost...and aware that Drew hadn't answered the question.

"And maybe want a chance to atone for what they did." Drew took the bottle away from Elliot's fingers, where they'd been peeling off the label. Elliot hadn't noticed.

"What *I* did, you mean. Being stupid and naïve, not realizing what kind of 'work' the firm did, and then turning a blind eye once I did?" Elliot gave a bitter laugh. "Oh, not that my father and uncle broke the law. Much. They used its loopholes to facilitate... questionable clients' needs, shall we say."

If Drew had looked into his background, he'd probably read all about the clients with overseas income and funds held in foreign banks in the name of an unnamed corporation, funds not disclosed to any tax authorities. Or perhaps Drew knew about the agents for government officials from high-risk jurisdictions who preferred to remain anonymous when they bought expensive property in the United States, property to be owned through corporations with undisclosed owners who benefited greatly from their real estate.

"What they advised, what they facilitated wasn't illegal," Elliot started, hating that he felt the compulsion to defend his father and uncle.

"I know anonymous shell companies aren't unlawful. They can be created for legitimate commercial reasons." Drew nudged the bottle of water nearer to Elliot to remind him to drink. "My unit's part of the Economic Crime Directorate, so we're well versed in those areas."

"Then you're probably also aware that using an offshore trust with an attorney acting as trustee to keep the source of the funds anonymous doesn't break any laws either."

"Is this what you told yourself at the time?" Drew asked.

Elliot dropped his gaze. It had been, yes, just as he'd reasoned that funneling clients' money through their firms' own bank accounts, though less usual was, again, not *illegal.* "Law firms aren't obliged to file suspicious activity reports in the same way as banks are," he continued. "And lawyers argue that their actions on behalf of their clients are part of their right to counsel."

"And your Bar Council agrees?" Drew asked.

"The American Bar Association? Yes. It hasn't penalized any lawyer yet for engaging in those activities. And it lobbies against any bills Congress tries to introduce that would make it law for agents who create companies for their clients to report beneficial ownership information to federal law enforcement." He gave a hollow laugh. "Yes, the ABA is the main roadblock to this reform—and my father and uncle are both very prominent members."

"Keeping the loophole open." Drew nodded.

He got it, of course. Drew was an expert in this area, but, more importantly, a shrewd judge of people, Elliot felt. He also sensed Drew's kindness, under the forcefulness that made him shiver to recall it. He went to explain more, but a tap at the door made him stop.

"Must be the food." Drew pulled on his shirt and crossed the room to deal with it. He was soon back at the desk with a loaded tray.

The food smelled good even before Drew removed the domes over the plates, and Elliot was surprised to find he was hungry. "You did order tea. And a jug of milk." He'd thought that was a joke and seeing the silver teapot now made him want to smile, despite all the other emotions coursing through him.

"And sugar lumps." Drew lifted the lid on the small bowl. "I'm not a doctor, but I'm prescribing you two. And just to repeat, I am sorry to bring all this painful history up."

Elliot found he believed him…and liked him for it. "Thank you." He accepted the cup of tea, the aromatic drink with milk and sugar taking him back to childhood. "I expect you have several questions, ranging from didn't I know to how long did I turn a blind eye to it once I did."

Drew finished pouring his own tea and set the pot down. "I'm not judging or making assumptions. I'd like you to tell me, if you can talk about it."

"It's actually something of a relief to talk about it," Elliot replied. So he did, describing the kind of clients Elliot & Elliot had handled, or facilitated…and taken a large cut from, the number of corporations set up in Nevada, Oregon and Wyoming, not to mention Delaware, the places with the loosest company formation and reporting requirements. It was a long story, told over the creamy scrambled eggs that were cooked with cheese and chives, he discovered.

"When I first learned the name 'shell company' it reminded me of 'shell game'," Drew said.

He served Elliot, and Elliot watched the play of Drew's muscles as he did so, his attentiveness only enhancing his virile masculinity. Drew had dark chest hair, visible in the gap of his mostly unbuttoned shirt, and Elliot wondered what it would feel like rubbing against his nipples.

He didn't get much out of nipple play—Drew had called that one correctly—but the thought of Drew's hair-roughened torso on them, or maybe his strong five-o-clock shadow scratching at them as he nipped and bit. If he dragged his bearded chin down Elliot's stomach, he'd— "Shell?" Elliot repeated, trying to keep up. To catch up.

"You know, that old thing played at fairgrounds, for instance, where the operator puts a pea under one of three shells, shuffles them around and the player has to say which holds the pea?"

Elliot laughed, enjoying the insight into Drew's thinking. "Yes. That's not really a game, but a confidence trick, done with sleight of hand."

"And lots of bells and whistles to convince potential players that the game's legit. The analogy holds." Drew sprinkled salt on his eggs and held the cruet over Elliot's, asking silently if he wanted any. Elliot shook his head. "So what removed the blinkers from your eyes?"

"Times changed and the family was changing with them. May I?" Elliot went to pour himself more tea, but Drew beat him to it, serving him and adding milk and sugar as before. Drew was a good Dom, attentive to his sub's needs. Elliot had seen a few at the club who didn't take care of serving their sub, the way Drew did, just expected the sub to service them.

Not that I'm his sub. Fine, so I was. But that doesn't mean I'd like to be again, now I know he lied to me and is probably blackmailing me. Except…I would. Elliot raised his cup to his lips and hid his confusion behind it.

"Things got to the point that working within the US wasn't enough. My father and uncle had expensive tastes and habits. I signed for a package from a courier one day and didn't notice it was for my uncle, just opened it absent-mindedly. I learned that he and my father had been working with a lawyer in Panama for a while—I had no idea—and were actually planning to set up an offshore branch of the firm there!"

"It's a tax haven," Drew commented. "Where high-rolling corporations and individuals go to avoid paying their fair share."

His lips thinned, and Elliot shifted—Drew's stern, almost brooding look was making Elliot's cock stir. And from Drew's reaction, it appeared that he felt like Elliot did about a system which allowed the wealthy and powerful to avoid paying what they owed to society. "And it's somewhere money coming from political corruption and fraud can be hidden," Elliot added, almost in a whisper.

Elliot & Elliot's Panama client roster would have included oligarchs and Middle Eastern royal families, some dodging sanctions, and some evading tax. The thought of his family helping the ruthless and avaricious had sickened Elliot, although he'd tried to understand how it had come about—the inevitable consequence of his greedy father and uncle chasing bigger and bigger game.

"It's also a place from where embezzled money is laundered." He didn't suppose he'd have to explain anything about that to Drew. "The FBI were interested in high-value real estate transactions in New York and London made by anonymous companies or straw purchasers, and with me not being complicit—my name not being on anything—I was granted immunity from prosecution in exchange for the information I provided."

Had his father's plan been to send Elliot to set up the Panama office, assuming he'd be a willing party? Elliot would never know but suspected as much. He'd tried to continue working in law afterward—the federal criminal investigator in charge of the case had helped him to find the attorney's office that had taken him on—but his heart hadn't been in it. He was lucky that the inheritance he'd gotten from his grandfather had enabled him to carve out a living in a field he loved.

"I'm sorry that your grandfather's name was tarnished," Drew said, making Elliot blink. They barely knew each other, and the darkly handsome man seemed able to discern what was important to him.

"I liked my name," he replied. "I loved him, yes, and didn't want to disassociate from my family. My brother has health problems that make it hard for him to connect to the world, and my sister never concerned herself with the business, so neither of them understand what I did or why I did it. They only know what Father told them about why he's not practicing as a lawyer any longer, and why he had to sell the mansion we grew up in. I miss them. All of them."

He'd changed their names too, in his mind, deciding not to tell anyone their real ones, in case someone put two and two together. The younger brother he'd known as Kit he now thought of as Chris, and his sister Natalia was no longer Tally, but Natty. Those were the versions of their names that he'd mentioned to Aldric and to Jonas recently when the subject of brothers and sisters had come up. Tiny details, but one never knew.

"I hope you get to see them soon." Drew set his knife and fork down on his plate, the fork with its tines down, English-style. "Elliot, we're similar, because that's what I'm doing, on the trail of this crook, stopping a thug profiting from theft. Could you help me?"

"How?" Elliot genuinely didn't understand.

"I need to track those paintings down, find out why they're so important to this man that he'd ship them here. I was making inquiries at the arts fair and didn't get any answers. Like any little world, the antiques circle here is a closed one, and I need a way in."

Before Elliot could protest at being used like that, Drew added, "And I'll use any pretext to see you again too. That scene was phenomenal. Your responses were— You're blushing? *Elliot!*"

"I am *not*," Elliot muttered, wanting to fan his heated face.

"I'd love to play again." Drew took his hand. "A week or so. That's all I'm asking—hell, it's all I've got."

Elliot opened his mouth to reply but his head nodded without him thinking about it or planning to do it. *Oh.* But his plans, to demolish the wall around himself brick by brick… *Seems the wall took a hit from a hurricane. An English hurricane.* Leaving him rocked to his foundations, and breathless.

Drew grinned, his teeth a white flash in the dark scruff of his beard. "And I have a follow-up question to ask you… I'd love to know how long you can still feel me for?"

Chapter Nine

Two days, Elliot could have told him, because that amount of time had passed and he could still feel Drew, the touch of his firm hand and the thrust of his hard cock. He was also still hearing that assured, commanding English voice telling him what he was going to do to Elliot, and what Elliot was going to take. If they got together again, what more would Drew do to him…force him to do? How far past his comfort zone would Drew push him? As far as Elliot…wanted him to?

"Elliot?"

It took him a second to realize that was an actual voice, in front of him in the store. *Aldric.*

"Anything wrong?" he asked, catching the wrinkle on his assistant's forehead.

"I was about to ask you that!" Aldric's big brown eyes, slightly magnified by his glasses, were wide with concern.

"Why?"

"Well, you were a little late this morning." Aldric bit down on his bottom lip. "Oh, I wasn't criticizing. That came out wrong. Sorry. What I meant was, you have a set routine and—"

"And now I'm deviating." *And how.* He never had hook-ups, didn't lead that sort of life. But he had and the connection was still zinging through him…even if it was bittersweet because it had made him crave more. He'd been telling himself all yesterday and today to be realistic, because what 'more' could he and Drew have? For all their amazing connection, the handsome, powerful Drew was a temporary visitor to the city, and Elliot's life. Oh, and a man who was openly using him, for God's sake!

"You're just standing here, near the window, gazing around the store." Aldric gestured. "Is there a problem with the window display here, or the stock?"

"No." Elliot sought for a reassuring smile. *I was simply lost in thoughts of the best fuck of my life, from which I'm still sore, and brooding about which is making me heartsore too.* "I'm simply being vain and admiring the place."

"That's not vain—Intrinsic Value is the best antiques shop in the city!" Aldric spoke with the firm conviction of fierce loyalty, and Elliot treasured that as much as any item on the premises. "Isn't it, Jonas?" he called to the store's third staff member, returning from the safe.

"Indeed it is," Jonas replied, equally faithful.

The place was very familiar to Elliot after so long, but as with any retail business, the changing nature of the goods meant the store was constantly renewed. He took in a deep breath, going beyond the tart citrus of the lemongrass room freshener to the cedar and camphor of the wooden chests here just inside the window.

They were open, the cedar displaying the clean stripes of vintage Hudson Bay blankets and the camphor chest a selection of even older darker-patterned Pendletons. He *wasn't* standing here because the aromatic woods reminded him of Drew's cologne, a sort of cedar with flintiness.

He turned away, thinking it better to fill his senses with something else. *Oh yes.* Elliot had acquired a set of heritage quilts that he'd thought of placing in one of the chests, but Aldric had exclaimed over the variety of squares and said the piece deserved to be *really* seen, so Elliot had displayed it by draping it artfully over a small table half in and half out of the shop window, and it did seem to bring in people eager to see it up close. Elliot planned to find an even nicer one to present to his employee and Darrell at their housewarming.

He caught the end of Aldric's proud glance at the quilt and roamed his gaze farther, to the hand-carved dresser that held a full set of brown and orange 1970s dinnerware. People catching a glimpse of that through the window had come in to exclaim over it and the memories of their childhood that it brought back, and Elliot had no doubt it would be gone by the end of the month.

Like Drew. He had less than two weeks for the assignment, if that was what they called these cases. Thinking of Drew working the case led Elliot to thoughts of Frank Heise, the FBI detective who'd set him on this path, which had brought him here, to Intrinsic Value. "Someone gave me a chance a few years ago and made this possible," Elliot muttered, recalling what he'd told Aldric when he'd taken a gamble on him by hiring him. With an effort, he pulled himself back into the present.

"I'm procrastinating," he told Aldric. "I've got research to do. I'm tracking down some specific artworks for a…person."

He went back to work in his office at the rear of the store, leaving the door open so he could see the shop. Even when he was busy, looking up at the treasures he'd collected and put together in displays soothed him. He flicked through another book of paintings, trying to find the exact ones he'd seen on the stall and wishing he had paid better attention. If he'd known it was so important…if he'd known he'd be working with Scotland Yard…

The very idea made him smile, as if he were in one of the detective stories his grandfather used to read to him, and the first editions of which Elliot had started collecting even back when he was still an attorney. And while the whole thing with Drew might seem fantastic, like the plot of a movie or TV show, the US having forty percent of the global art market provided a large arena for crime. Elliot had witnessed that in all its rough, gritty brutality at the Southtown events center.

He started another phone call to a dealer, hoping this one wouldn't be pressing him for details about the stabbing and robbery at the fair. It still made him shudder to recall the incident. How did law enforcement cope with such horror?

"Elliot…" His door was open, but Aldric knocked on the jamb. "You have a visitor!" His voice was almost singing with excitement.

Confused, Elliot recapped his pen after having made notes on his latest unsuccessful call and looked up…to see Drew. *Here? Why?* He wondered if his face was heating as much as Aldric's was, and Aldric's was second-hand.

"Oh, hello," he greeted Drew, coming out from behind his desk to shake his hand. He didn't get the chance.

With a firm, "You can do better than that," and a gleam in his blue-gray eyes, Drew pulled him into a hard hug, and his eyes glinted more when Drew's cock instantly stirred.

Elliot caught sight of not just Aldric but Jonas hovering in the doorway. "This is Andrew Harrington. My employees and friends Aldric Beamer and Jonas Abrams." He was careful not to mention Drew's connection to him as the trio shook hands. "Is there something you wanted?" he asked his staff.

The way the other two were still there suggested there was, although Elliot wanted to ask Drew the same question too. Drew knew where Elliot worked—they'd exchanged contact information, and Elliot had planned to call Drew's cell phone later that evening. *With a progress report. Not hoping for anything. Certainly not another unbelievably good session involving bondage or—*

"It's the lunch today," Aldric half-whispered.

"Of course it is." Elliot turned to Drew, standing still and commanding attention in the too-full, too-small office. "Cabot's, the restaurant across the square, is holding a thanks day and rewarding loyal local customers with free starters and drinks."

"Oh, I'm intruding. I won't stay long." Drew's voice was even better than Elliot remembered and his woodsy, gunmetal cologne much sexier.

"No, it's fine." Elliot wondered where his employees were rushing off to, leaving him and Drew alone. Being alone with this man was dangerous.

"I've been calling your mobile—sorry, cell—but it goes to voice mail, and the office line's been engaged. I didn't want to call the main number for the store." Drew glanced at the doorway. "I came to show you this, or have you seen it?" Drew held out his phone for Elliot to see the screen. "On Craigslist?"

"I've heard of it," Elliot replied, squinting at the text. "The list, I mean. But what—?"

"Mr. Cabot says one extra's no problem!" Aldric almost sang from the doorway, making Elliot jump. "Mr. Harrington can come to lunch too!" And for someone so sweet and shy, Aldric could be stubborn when he wanted to be, and this was clearly one of those times.

Aldric backed up by Darrell, who arrived a minute or so later to join them, made protest impossible and the small party walked the short distance to the brasserie where a very long table in the middle of the restaurant was reserved for an assorted group of regulars from the surrounding businesses and stores.

"*Sorry,*" Elliot mouthed to Drew as they were swept along in the tide. This felt nerve-wracking to him, so how was Drew taking it?

In stride, seemed to be the answer. "I love a midweek party," he assured Elliot and those of his staff who were eavesdropping. "And what a great place." He took in the long brasserie's exposed beams and stone floors. "Was it a factory?"

"Probably a brewery," Elliot replied.

"Apt for a brasserie," Drew quipped in reply, and Elliot laughed. He'd been using the place for a few years and had forgotten that *brasserie* was indeed French for brewery. He loved that Drew, who emanated control and focus, had a sense of humor.

He was unable to keep the smile from tilting his lips when Drew pulled out his seat for him and waited for him to sit. He didn't miss Meredith, the restaurant's delivery assistant, elbowing Aldric to make sure he caught it too, *and* the way that Drew settled next to him. Meredith brought meals to Intrinsic Value at least twice a week and was friendly with all three of its staff. Elliot was pleased to see she was a guest at this event too, being thanked for her work at Cabot's. She joined their section of the table, subtly jostling to sit beside Drew, but losing to Aldric.

Elliot could only hope they wouldn't be too intrusive in asking the questions that were almost visible on their lips.

"Mr. Harrington," Aldric began, giving a cough to get his voice working normally. Afflicted with anxiety and shyness, he didn't let them stand in his way when he wanted something. "Are you a new client of the store?"

"Call me Drew, please. All of you." Drew made sure he caught the eye of their party. "I'm new here, yes. What I've seen of the city so far is interesting and this part especially—it seems a great area to wander around in. I envy you all working here. Why I'm here is that I'm interested in paintings by a group of American artists, but I'm not a client myself."

Elliot had to admire his smooth non-lie. He could see Aldric and Jonas categorizing Drew as a middleman, a buyer for other people.

"And before you ask, I only met Elliot recently, at the art and antiques fair here in town." His eyes shone more blue than gray as he dealt with their curiosity. "We went out for a drink and..." He finished in a shrug.

He forced me to take what I craved and dominated the hell out of me. Elliot pasted what he hoped was a bland smile on his face in case any of those thoughts showed through. He greeted Bill Cabot, the owner, and tried to relax, nodding as the stout, red-faced man welcomed everyone and listed today's hot and cold *entrées* and *hors-d'oeuvres* of soups, salads, sandwiches and omelets that they were all welcome to.

"Still think your idea to eat three or four starters and get a free meal that way is a go?" Darrell teased Aldric.

"No," he replied. "Not now I can smell the pizzas and burgers."

"How long are you in town for?" Darrell suddenly asked Drew, leaning forward over Aldric to address him.

"Darrell!" Aldric squealed. "It sounds like you're interrogating him!"

"Patrol Officer Williams is with the San Antonio Police Department," Elliot informed Drew. Damn! He should have mentioned it.

"Oh?" Drew assessed Darrell, and Elliot wondered what he was thinking. "I'm here for less than a fortnight."

"Like…the game?" Darrell asked, his forehead corrugating.

"Fortnight is British for two weeks," Elliot translated.

"Thank you." The half-smile Drew sent his way had Elliot weak. "Then back to London."

"What's England like?" Aldric asked, his tone wistful.

"Hm." Drew tilted his head, taking the measure of Aldric. "Why don't you tell me what you *think* it's like, and I'll tell you how near the mark you are?"

Answers came thick and fast to this, ranging from everything being small, to it raining all the time, to everyone being clever and snooty, like professors. Drew laughed, assuring Meredith that while they *did* take their soft drinks, or sodas, a little warmer than here, they *did* have ice cubes.

Elliot would have joined in the laughter, but he was focusing on breathing normally…because Drew had dropped his hand onto his thigh and was moving it upward in a slow and sensuous stroke. Elliot stared down at his plate, not daring to meet anyone's eye. If Drew moved his hand a little higher, he'd find how Elliot was not only stirring but stiffening, if he didn't know already.

Drew's casual mastery over him in public like this shocked Elliot to the core. How had Drew discerned it was a dark, deep-hidden fantasy of his? *He hasn't, you idiot,* Elliot told himself. *He's keeping up the pretense that we're dating so I can help him with the case.*

And it worked in that no one seemed suspicious when Drew accompanied them back to the store, having passed their tests and met with their approval.

"Sorry again for that," Elliot apologized when they were alone in his office, the door firmly closed.

"Don't be. I'm not. I enjoy spending time with you. Just wish it was under other circumstances." Drew fished out his phone. "Here's the ad."

"Newly acquired original sea painting for sale. Oil. Signed M H Heade…" Elliot squinted at the screen. "This could be one of the paintings from the fair, yes!"

"Do you know the seller, Sanchez?"

"No, I don't know any dealer or trader by that name." Elliot lifted the receiver of his rotary phone and dialed. "Oh, good afternoon. Mr. Sanchez?"

The grunt he received in reply wasn't exactly encouraging, but he plowed on. "My name's Elliot Douglas, and I'm an antiques trader—you may know my shop, Intrinsic Value?" Silence met this. "I'm interested in the oil painting you're selling and wonder if you could bring it to my store for a viewing? Any time is fine— No? But— Really? That's—"

The buzzing on the line meant that the man had disconnected.

"What?" Drew demanded as Elliot hung up.

"He won't bring it here. He says I'm to go there, to him, to the address he gave, this evening."

From the set of Drew's shoulders, this wasn't usual, and from the way he was about to speak, he was going to tell Elliot that he'd take it from here. *Fine.* This was outside Elliot's skill set now. He'd helped Drew out, as he'd agreed, and this was now Drew's pigeon.

Except…that meant Elliot would have no reason to meet with Drew again and that realization landed like a blow.

So, never mind his skill set—maybe it was time Elliot worked outside his *comfort zone…*

Chapter Ten

Drew cast another glance out of the driver's-side window at the evening streets around them, then caught Elliot's eye in the mirror. "I still don't think this is a good idea. And no, it wasn't necessarily a problem you giving your real name and place of business. I could have posed as you, although I hardly imagine the seller will be quizzing me on the finer points of the arts and antiques trade or aspects of running a business."

He didn't like Elliot being along with him, although he'd meant what he said about enjoying spending time with him. *Who wouldn't?* The man was interesting, knowledgeable and witty, and his buttoned-up submission was so fucking sexy it had Drew slavering. Even thinking about the other night in his hotel room had him harder than he'd been most times in bed with Ash. Drew flexed his right hand—it could still feel the impact from spanking Elliot's ass.

But mixing work with, well, anything else—Drew never did that. He compartmentalized. Prioritized work. Meeting Elliot had him scrambled, and he didn't like it.

But if Elliot had to be along for this—and Drew still wasn't clear on why he'd insisted—at least he was dressed less formally, leaving off the three-piece suit and polished dress shoes for a sweater and slacks. He looked good in both…and better in nothing. Drew pulled up at the end of the street from their destination. "I think you should stay in the car," he said. He'd been crazy to agree to him coming this far.

"In this area?" Elliot scoffed. "Look."

Drew followed where Elliot was pointing. A cluster of kids hanging out under a streetlamp were already showing interest in the car Drew had hired, for all it was at the lower end of mid-range. He got out and studied the group, pinpointing the leader.

"Hey, you," he called. "Tall guy with black hair." He beckoned.

The guy sauntered over. "Want something?" he asked, his gaze flickering from Drew to Elliot, who was exiting the car.

"Yeah. This vehicle is to be in the same place and condition when I come back as it is now," Drew replied, standing still in front of the guy until he dropped eye contact.

"We all want stuff," the kid muttered.

"How about a fifty?"

Drew turned at Elliot's voice to see him sliding a bill from his pocket. He ripped it in two and held out half to the bewildered boy. "You get the rest when we return," he said.

The kid stood and stared.

"You heard him," Drew threw in.

Shrugging, the kid took the half-bill and strolled back to his gang, putting as much cool as he could into every step.

Drew raised an eyebrow at Elliot's old-school move. "I'm not buying that you secretly grew up on the streets," he said. Not when he knew exactly where and how Elliot had lived before moving to San Antonio.

Elliot waved a hand, looking a little embarrassed. "I watch old movies."

Drew was still suppressing a smile at that, and the many *fascinating* layers to this man when they reached the address Sanchez had given. It was one of a small grouping of apartment buildings around a forecourt, and a trio of sweatpants-and-hoodie-wearing, shaven-headed musclemen were clearly acting as security at its entrance. "My police instincts are screaming. What's available here? Drugs?" he mused.

"Weapons too, in this neighborhood," Elliot replied.

Yep. He'd figured that.

"Evening. How may we direct your visit?" asked one of the trio, sarcasm dripping from him.

"Sanchez," Drew replied.

"Apartment B3." The middle guy pointed to the second building from the right. "Nowhere else. Understood? We'll be watching."

Drew stepped into his space until the man swung aside for them to pass. "Understood."

He wondered if Elliot could feel the guys' eyes on them as they crossed the parking lot. The rundown apartment building's main door was propped open by a half-brick, making their entrance easy. Inside, he caught Elliot's arm so he didn't trip on the discarded trash littering the floor, or bang into any of the pipes sticking out from the crumbling wall. The noise of a TV came loud from one apartment, and a dog was barking and a child wailing in another.

"Still want to do this?" he murmured to Elliot, who gave him a firm nod, took a breath and started up the stairs.

The first apartment on the next story up had a thick, sturdy door and a series of locks. Drew rapped on it. "Sanchez? It's the buyer interested in the painting," he called.

The locks were opened, one by one, to reveal a man who was older and more unkempt than the usual petty crook Drew dealt with, but who gave off the same opportunist sneak-thief vibe. He narrowed his eyes at them and spoke to Drew. "Who're you?"

"Muscle." Drew folded his arms.

Sanchez made a scoffing noise, which became a cough, and let them in. Goods occupied every surface of the small room, from jewelry and watches along the windowsill to cell phones on a sideboard to laptops on a coffee table. Rows of canvases, prints and pictures, were stacked along one wall, with an oil seascape in the center of the outside row, as if newly placed. Elliot crouched to look at it at once.

"This is it, yes?" he asked Sanchez, who nodded.

"It's quite *stunning*." Elliot gave the code they'd arranged to let Drew know it was the one they were after. "Do you have any others similar? Landscapes, perhaps?" He was flicking through the front row of paintings as he spoke. "Apart from these? There are no others as *stunning*," he commented.

"Got what's there." Sanchez pointed a foot at the display.

"Where did you get it?" Elliot asked.

"Found it." The petty crook sniffed.

He wasn't going to be drawn into revealing anything, and Drew doubted that the guy had anything to reveal. He'd hoped Sanchez would lead them to something bigger, but this stooped, unwell, middle-aged man in this decrepit apartment was worlds apart from Kislyak's smooth villainy and the pitiless raiders from the fair.

He pivoted and grabbed Sanchez, pushed him against a peeling wall and cuffed him before the man had time to react. Drew eased off enough to retrieve his ID and slide it between the wall and Sanchez' face, allowing him just enough time to see Drew was law enforcement. "You're involved in something very big," he said. "Still claim you 'found' that painting?"

"I don't know nothing, man! I found it in the fucking street," Sanchez protested.

"Of course you did. Which street, when?" Drew jerked the cuffs, making his prisoner's arms strain.

"Southtown, outside that new event center. Few days ago."

"Someone just left it lying around?" Drew scorned.

"No, they dropped it when they were throwing stuff into a van. Some gang raided the hall and that was part of their haul.

"Who?" asked Elliot. "Which gang?"

"I don't know. Don't know nothing about gangs. Didn't see their faces neither. But they had to get clear and left the picture they dropped. Didn't go back for it. I was hanging around there and saw it. Thought I'd make money off it."

Thieves gotta thieve. Drew believed the guy. He had no connection to the art world. Was there any more to be learned here? Shouts and thuds from outside stopped his train of thought.

"What's that?" Elliot asked.

Drew tried to interpret the noises. "The security guards doing their job under difficult circumstances," he replied.

"But it sounds like it's just outside this building." Elliot looked from the door to Drew.

"Whether it is or isn't, we're out of here. Now. Where's the other exit? he demanded of Sanchez. Because there would be one.

Sanchez waggled his hands, his message clear. Drew snapped the cuffs free.

"Through there." Sanchez jerked his head.

"And we were never here. Just like you don't know anything about the gang who raised the exhibition hall, you didn't see us, either…if you want to stay clear of the cops." Drew glared for as many seconds as he could spare, then grabbed the painting and nudged Elliot into the other room.

It was a bedroom, as grim as the first room, but had a fire escape. Even if it hadn't, they were only two flights up so could have gotten out anyway. *Maybe not easily, carrying a painting in a frame, though.* Drew hurried behind Elliot down the zig, then the zag, of the rusty stairs.

The rear of the apartment complex was worse than the front, the small paved space strewn with thrown-out furniture and appliances as well as litter. The emergency gate in the wall enclosing it was chained shut.

Elliot stood and listened. "I think it *was* that building, the one we were just in."

Drew thought so too. He had to act quickly. "Hold this." Thrusting the painting at Elliot, he raced to push a battered old couch along the wall a few yards, in the direction of the unusable metal gate, then strained to upend it.

"We're going that way?" Elliot asked.

"No, this." Drew retrieved the picture and grabbed Elliot's hand, hustling him in the opposite direction, right up against the far wall, to crouch behind a short row of overflowing dumpsters there. They had barely ducked down before footsteps slammed on the metal fire escape steps and, from around his screen, Drew glimpsed two figures dressed in black coming to a halt then heading for the couch Drew had moved, to climb it and jump over the wall.

"Oh, clever!" Elliot exclaimed, peeping through a gap between dumpsters.

"Save the compliments for when we're at the car again," Drew told him, hoping that if the two men were engaged in pursuit along the streets behind the apartment complex in *that* direction, he and Elliot could retrace their steps in the other, and escape *this* way. "Come on."

"One second…" Elliot pulled a cotton square from his pocket, unfolded it and shook it out to make it into a large bag with cloth handles. He placed the painting in it. "There."

Drew was still mentally shaking his head at Elliot's level of preparation even as he helped him over the wall behind the trash containers and vaulted over himself. He took the bag.

"Do you think things will be all right?" Elliot asked as they jogged.

Drew understood what he was asking. "I think we'll make it back to the vehicle okay," was all he could answer. He was glad when their circular route took them around to the street where they'd left the car, and where the same group of teens loitered. Shouts from behind a low one-story house on the other side of the street had him nudging Elliot to rush—the property would be on the route of a short cut to this street, if anyone was following them.

The car unlocked and started fine—it didn't seem that the gang had pulled an ignition or fuel pump fuse, for instance.

"Thanks," Elliot called to the group of kids as Drew drove slowly past them. He fished out the other half of the fifty to hand over.

Drew doubted the group was saying complimentary things about them in their wake. He didn't relax until they'd left the west side of the city and were back on streets more familiar to Drew. That had been stupid. "You okay?" he snapped at Elliot, angry with himself that he'd let the situation happen. However much his adolescence and career had left him burning to bring rich crooks to justice, exposing a person he cared about to the underworld was— *Cared about?* He'd only just met the guy! *And you can't stop thinking about him,* a voice that sounded a bit like that of his partner, Claire, nagged at him.

"Elliot, you okay?" Drew repeated, wanting his conscience salved.

Elliot looked okay. More than, his eyes were bright and his cheeks flushed in a way that had Drew's breath catching, because it brought to mind Elliot's other cheeks that he wanted to see a bright pink color. *Want to turn that shade.*

"Yes. I think so." Elliot turned to him. "Where to now?"

Somewhere I can smack your ass hard then fuck it harder. Somewhere I'll have you on your knees to me…then have you. "Somewhere we can examine this painting," Drew said.

Elliot gave a tiny nod. "I-I know just the place."

Chapter Eleven

Elliot's courage and confidence evaporated the deeper they got into the Lavaca neighborhood. This was as bad an idea as him accompanying Drew had been. "We're here," he said, keeping his voice calm and neutral.

Drew parked and peered out. "I assumed you meant the store, until you directed me a different way, and then I presumed an artist's studio somewhere, maybe, but…this is your house, right?"

"Yes." Elliot exited the car then led Drew up the steps to the front door set at one end of the pillared porch, wondering if it were a bad or good thing that Drew could tell he owned the Robin's-egg blue and dove-gray property.

"It's Victorian?" Drew took in the house that Elliot had taken pains to keep from being too dollhouse-like. "Back home, they're more gloomy and dark with pointed bits. Not this pretty blue with nicely shaped windows."

"It's folk Victorian, so no towers, turrets and as few gables as possible. Plain construction with decorative trim." Elliot tilted his head at the off-white porch, and, farther back, at the roof line, with its darker-colored accents, to show Drew what he meant.

"Hey." Drew's hand on his arm stopped Elliot as he went to insert his key in the door. "I feel this is a big deal. I'd ask if you inherited the property, perhaps from your grandparents, but I know they had no connection with this city. Did you buy it and restore it? It means a lot to you, right?"

Again, how well Drew seemed to know him staggered Elliot. Maybe all detectives were intuitive or empathetic? "Yes. It's not finished. I'm trying…" *To make it as perfect as possible.* "It's a work in progress."

"Isn't everything…including people?" Drew answered, looking around the hall Elliot showed him into, then back at Elliot. His words struck Elliot, as did the way his gaze lingered, as though he saw more than the prim, old-fashioned façade Elliot Douglas presented to the world, through to the man underneath—a man with complex needs and desires he'd only recently come to understand and barely begun to act upon.

Elliot nodded, slowly. "Yes. Well, I'm pleased to welcome you to my home." He rushed into speech, to cover up how charged, how significant things felt. "Cute but hopefully not cloying is what I'm going for, inside and out. I'm doing it room by room."

"That must be interesting and rewarding."

"I'm going to have people over, have a housewarming, when it's finished." *Whenever that might be.*

Drew's half-smile could be read as him catching that stray thought, and being amused by it, as if he knew Elliot considering it finished was a long way off. He whistled his appreciation at the winding wooden staircase they passed.

"You're the first person to see the place," Elliot blurted out.

"Really?" Drew's face registered his surprise. "Then thank you. I'm honored." He followed Elliot into the living room. "I'm only sorry I'm not better able to appreciate it. I like the big rooms and high ceilings and that it looks spacious and not cluttered." He laughed. "As you can see, that's the level of my architectural or design knowledge. But you have some lovely bits and bobs."

Hearing a British expression his grandfather had used made Elliot laugh. "I do, including some actual drill bits and screwdriving bobs in my toolbox," he couldn't help replying, riffing on the humor they seemed to share. He led Drew into the dining room he was in the middle of working on, where benches and trestle tables held a range of equipment and materials, wondering at the slow and dirty grin hitching up Drew's lips.

"You realize this is fodder for sexy construction worker fantasies, right?" Drew pointed at the bench. "The tool…*belt*, the hard…*hat*…"

Elliot chuckled again. "Sorry I can't play along—I get specialists in for all that and just do the smaller, easier parts."

Did Drew understand how much all this represented him, everything planned and ordered, each stage projected, scheduled and monitored, to keep it all under control…and yet how the whole thing felt if not empty, then not enough?

It wasn't that he wanted to punch a fist through the painstakingly hand-turned balusters stair spindles, or take a hammer to the carefully collected ceiling and wall lights. Everything he was doing, or trying to do, with the house was important to him…but it was just one part of him. There were other facets. Other more basic, primal and raw needs. He went to turn away, but Drew stopped him.

Drew pulled him close, his hand holding Elliot's head to his chest. Elliot heard the thump of Drew's heart beneath his ear for a second before he felt a kiss pressed onto the top of his head. Drew released him almost immediately and looked startled by his action too.

"Thank you for letting me see you," he said, his already deep voice a little gruffer. "And now, shall we move onto another work of art?"

Not knowing if Drew's appreciation referred to the house or maybe, possibly, him, Elliot gave a nod. "Of course."

His equipment for restoration work was in here, so there were plenty of pairs of gloves to don. He took the cotton bag Drew was still toting and eased the artwork free, to take it to the table where his white-light lamp stood.

"The paint's on the other side of that," Drew commented, when Elliot held the painting to the light and looked at the back. "What do you see?" Drew asked.

"Nothing. And in an original piece, you'd see the light passing through in spots where the paint was applied less heavily. This is very uniform. The back tells you just as much as the front when it comes to authentication." Elliot felt a little smug.

"Hm, and talking of the back, I'd say the biggest clue is that the canvas and stretcher bars are white, with no oxidation." Drew indicated the tiny wooden struts but didn't touch them.

"Clue to it being a forgery." Elliot sighed. "Yes, I think it is. I'm sorry, Drew."

"No, that's good! May I?" Drew snagged a pair of gloves and pulled them on. He helped himself to a small knife and, with immense care, eased it into a corner of the frame and pulled. Before Elliot's astonished eyes, the wooden frame gave and came toward Drew…bringing the painting with it. The top painting, that was. Because underneath the seascape was another picture, this also depicting water—a river and a bridge.

Elliot's jaw dropped at the soft subtle blues and grays of the sky and water. The painting gave the impression of light captured and— "Impressionist!" He gasped. "Is that a *Monet*? An actual, real *Monet*?"

"I believe so." Drew's gaze was glued to the canvas. "One of his *London Bridge* series, stolen from a small modern art gallery in Paris. Let's just hope whoever put the new backing onto this priceless work of art didn't damage it."

"I don't think I understand." Elliot was sure he didn't. He peeled off his gloves.

"I haven't explained fully." Drew slowly let the fake painting and the frame fall into place again, hiding the beauty beneath. "I'm not exactly tracking stolen Americana. I wondered why the suspect had such paintings hanging in his house, works he made sure to let us see. Well, that part was him laughing in our faces, thinking we had no idea he'd be using forged art to hide real stolen art, when he shipped it to buyers in the US."

Elliot swallowed. "And you can prove it?"

Drew removed his gloves and pulled out his phone. "I shot these photos of the American paintings in his penthouse. Even got one of his servants in, look, as extra evidence. I have copies of his shipping manifests from London to here. And now this. So, one down, two to go."

Knowing Drew wasn't rushing back to London tonight filled Elliot with relief. "We can't leave this here, in the open," he said, indicating the artwork.

"Do you have a home safe?" Drew queried.

"Yes. This way." Elliot led Drew along the corridor to the back of the house and the short set of steps leading down to what had been a pantry, but what was now a state-of-the-art walk-in safe in the basement. They placed the cotton bag with care in a free corner. "I'll activate the locks." Elliot wanted to get Drew out of this area.

Drew, of course, halted at the door on the far side of the room. "The rest of this basement…" he said. "May I see it?"

"Oh, well, it's not finished." Elliot tried to lead Drew away.

"Elliot."

That firm voice stopped him in his tracks.

"That's not what I asked. Open this door, please."

Shoulders drooping, Elliot activated the keypad to open the door…to his playroom. Or would-be playroom, if he had a partner to play with. A line from a movie flashed across his mind—*If you build, they will come.* No, it had been blind hope that had propelled this move. He switched on the heating and the spotlights.

"I see." Drew turned in a slow circle, taking in the bench and equipment of a different nature to those upstairs. "It looks finished enough to me. Was that a lie?"

"I... Yes." Elliot stood with his gaze averted, until Drew's hand raised his chin for him.

"Your kink is rough sex in which your partner dominates you. There's no shame in that."

"I'm not ashamed. Just..."

"Not comfortable with it," Drew finished for him.

"No. Not exactly." Elliot blew out a breath. The world saw him as the prim overdressed antiques trader he presented as, but that was only a part of who he was. "I like being told what to do in sex but that doesn't make me weak or broken," he got out in a rush, trying to explain.

"And I like telling a guy what to do during sex, but that doesn't make me a jerk. And I don't want anyone weak or damaged. Well, only the 'damage' I inflict." Drew gave a slow lick of his lips, and Elliot followed the motion, his dick hardening. "I understand, Elliot. It's like two sides to a coin. You're self-contained, with everything meticulously planned. It's how you control your life. But you also need relief. Release. What happened between us the other day proved that."

He understands me. This was becoming more and more evident the more they interacted. Of course Drew would understand these facets to a person. Elliot wondered if Drew being a Dom had to do with his life, his job—he needed to have control and he must compartmentalize a great deal. Before Elliot could ponder on it any further, Drew was speaking again.

"If you haven't had visitors to the house, does that mean no one else has been in here?"

Elliot nodded. He didn't trust easily and there was no one he knew well enough, or he felt knew *him* well enough to bring here. There was Karl, of course, but this wouldn't come under the services he provided.

"Then I'm the lucky one—" Drew began, although Elliot felt he was, to have had that night with Drew. The thought that there would be more of what they'd shared had his pulse racing.

"—who gets to break it in," Drew said, and Elliot, almost light-headed, heard it as *break you in*. Drew had indeed done that. Where Elliot had watched scenes at Caress and wanted to submit to a Dom, he hadn't been able to make himself...but Drew had made him, made Elliot submit to him and to whatever Drew had chosen to do to him. And Elliot had fucking loved it.

"Still the same?"

Elliot pulled himself from his reverie and breathed through the haze of arousal to attend to what Drew must have inquired of him.

"I said, are they still the same? I asked you a question." Drew was still holding Elliot's face.

"What? I was dreaming, sorry."

Those fingers now tightened. "Pay more attention. Are your safewords and signals the same?"

"Yes."

"I mentioned fucking your face before, and you looked like a kid at a party." Drew's tone was conversational, as if this were nothing out of the ordinary. "Condoms for oral or not? I got tested recently and I'm clean. I've got the results on my phone somewhere if you'd like to see."

"I... No. Bare." Even the word sent a thrum along Elliot's nerve endings. *Raw.* God, the mere thought had him leaking pre-cum.

"And you take a load? To the face? Swallow?"

Jesus. All Elliot could do was nod, his eyes widened so much that his forehead hurt.

"Good." Drew dropped his hand from Elliot's face and prowled the basement room. "It's well-stocked," he commented.

Elliot kept quiet, limiting himself to nodding. Drew was sharpening, gathering himself together...for their scene, and Elliot was almost hyperventilating.

"So go get a mat." Drew waited for Elliot to obey him. "Now, on your knees. Get me ready."

Chapter Twelve

Elliot dropped to his knees and couldn't help but flinch when Drew unbuckled his belt. He tracked the movement with his gaze. *No. His belt?* Would Drew— And did Elliot want him too? His dick was certainly intrigued by the thought, straining against his pants. This, him on his knees, spot lit in his newly fitted-out dungeon in front of a Dom, felt so...*right,* was the adjective his brain settled on.

This looked like becoming a more elaborate scene than the one they'd had in Drew's hotel room, but that, Drew pounding his ass, had been perfect in its own way too. Drew unzipped his jeans, and Elliot almost exclaimed to see he wasn't wearing underwear, then couldn't bite back his gasp at how hard Drew's cock was when Drew took it out.

Drew had no problem understanding Elliot's non-verbal communication. "How could I not be hard, with your eager mouth an inch away?" he remarked. "Hands behind your back. I want *just* your mouth."

Elliot complied, his gaze drinking in the sight of Drew's erect cock, long and fat with a vein he wanted to lick running up the side, almost to the thick flare of its head. He inhaled, filling his nostrils with the salty, musky scent that had his head swimming. Drew held the base in one hand.

"Jesus, you're licking your lips!" he exclaimed.

Elliot didn't know if Drew meant that as a metaphor or he'd actually swiped his tongue over them. He opened his mouth to ask, and Drew chose that moment to ease the tip of his cock between Elliot's lips.

"Lick this instead," he ordered.

Elliot did, learning its taste and texture, that he could circle it with the flat of his tongue and that if he wriggled his tongue tip into the slit, he could scoop out pre-cum to sip and swallow. Every so often, Drew pulled out to either swipe his cock along Elliot's lips or smack his cheek with it. Both actions felt so dirty and so good and not enough...but he got no warning before Drew pushed in, this time right to the back of his throat, and that was too much. Elliot's throat spasmed.

"Can't take much, can you?" Drew remarked. "Try harder."

Elliot did his best, opening wide and taking Drew in as deep as he could go. He choked, and his eyes watered, the tears slipping down his burning cheeks.

"I'm going easy on you," came Drew's voice above him, as he fucked Elliot's throat with long, slow pushes and pulls. "Mainly because I like the noises you make."

He likes the gagging sounds I'm half-ashamed of? Oh.

"But you can't take it all, can you? Look at me." Drew made his order easier to obey by spearing his fingers into Elliot's hair and pulling him free of his shaft.

Drew shook his head, a couple of tears that had leaked from his eyes flicking off and onto the matt under his knees.

"Then we have work to do. Training to do," Drew said, a smirk twisting his face. He rammed his dick in before Elliot was expecting it, making him choke. "Yeah, those noises." He slid the hand he'd tightened in Elliot's hair lower, to hold the back of his head, keeping him where he wanted him, and that added restraint had Elliot almost coming where he knelt.

He adjusted, breathing through his nose so he didn't feel as though a lack of oxygen would make him pass out, although it wasn't that which was making him feel heady.

"You're doing well," Drew commented, and the praise rained down on Elliot like a gift from the gods. "And I'm getting the feel of you now."

Which meant he increased his pace…and the force of his thrusts. It pulled lewd, wet slurping noises from Elliot's mouth, and Drew chuckled. "I like those noises too. Jesus, but I love going hard. Really *hammering* a sub's throat, seeing what they can take…and making them take… That. Bit. More."

His words sent a charge up Elliot's spine. Sweat dewed his body, especially his hands, making it impossible for him to keep them clasped together behind his back. His arms sprang to the sides then the front, and he gripped the back of Drew's legs to keep in position.

Oh, this was much better. Before he knew what he was planning to do, he slid his hands under the denim of Drew's jeans so he could wrap his hands around Drew's skin. He only knew he must have dug the nails of one hand in when Drew hissed in reaction. It wasn't the ideal position for Elliot—his balance and stability were off, and he felt unsteady…probably the way Drew liked him.

Maybe in retaliation for Elliot's unauthorized foray, Drew picked up speed, shoving his cock deep over and over again until Elliot cried out around the flesh filling his mouth and throat.

"Need to take a breath?" Drew asked, sounding mildly amused, and Elliot gave the tiniest shake of his head, determined to take it all, all that Drew could give him. He was too focused on timing his breathing with Drew's out-strokes to be embarrassed about the saliva dripping in a dirty string from his mouth and down his face.

"Look at me," Drew suddenly demanded, and if that was hard, staring into Drew's eyes as he fucked Elliot's mouth, dealing with his question when he asked, "You ready to swallow my load?" was even tougher. Drew must have known that, understood how the picture he was painting sent fear and anticipation and desire coursing through Elliot.

It was like winning the lottery when Drew halted. He held himself deep in Elliot's mouth, and his iron hand around Elliot's head kept his face buried in Drew's crotch, his nose in his pubic hair.

"I'm the one who needs a breather, or this is gonna be over too soon," Drew panted. He used his other hand to pull Elliot's hair. "You're a quick learner and look so fucking hot on your knees with my dick down your throat that I want to show you off. I think I will, take you to a club and show everyone what a fantastic cocksucker you are."

Elliot froze, his breath sawing from his lungs in terrified gulps. The tears trickling from his eyes were now ones of panic. Drew relaxed his grip on Elliot's head and pulled his face back, leaving the tip of his cock throbbing on Elliot's tongue as he looked at him. He was bluffing, wasn't he? He wouldn't make Elliot perform in public, in either the main room or one of the small side rooms at Caress, let people see him sucking Drew off? *Would he?*

"You might wanna take your last deep breath," Drew warned, giving him a second before he pushed Elliot's head down again. "Because I'm gonna come in your mouth, and you're gonna swallow me down. Word of advice—try to control your gag reflex now."

Elliot's fingers, still clutching on to the lifeline of Drew's legs, tightened. He didn't quite know what to expect and there was no time to imagine, because Drew clamped his hands around Elliot's head to hold him in place for Drew to thrust deep and jerk Elliot back and forth, quick and short, on his dick. His agonized shout warned Elliot a second before Drew gave one last deep roll of his hips and jetted into his mouth.

He was going to choke. To drown. On Drew's thick, warm, salty-sweet cum shooting down his throat. Thankfully, Drew pulled out a little, holding the base of his cock, so the next pulse pooled on Elliot's tongue, and he was able to suck, as hard as he could—hard enough to make Drew groan.

He didn't understand when Drew slid his still-throbbing shaft free of Elliot's mouth, making his lips close on nothing as he chased it, not wanting to lose it.

"Yeah, there's more," Drew gritted out. "And I want to see you dripping with it. With me." He slid his hand up his still-swollen, still-red dick, and moaned as he worked it hard and fast, to pull the rest of his climax from it—and shoot his load right into Elliot's face. If the splat noise it made hitting him was obscene, the heavy, wet warmth sliding down his skin was even more so. Although he'd had Drew's cock down his throat, had sucked the cum from it, he had to stick out his tongue and taste these pulses of it too.

Elliot had never seen anything like Drew's face above him as he milked out the last spasms. Which made him wonder—what did he look like, heaving as if he'd run a race, his face as red as fire, his hair one sweat-soaked mass, his lips parted, Drew's release dripping from his chin?

"Fucking gorgeous," Drew rasped out, making Elliot fret that he'd voiced his question out loud. "Covered in me—fucking gorgeous."

Elliot could have come right from those words alone. Now that he didn't have to concentrate on breathing without choking, his urgent need to release wracked him. He was actually shaking with the intensity of it, wanting to rock back and forth with the pain.

Drew understood. Of course he did—he'd created this, fed it, made it blaze out of control. "Get yourself off," he ordered, groping out a hand and dragging over a stool. The noise its legs made, scraping over the floor, hit Elliot hard in his heightened state. But the stool wasn't for him—it was for Drew to collapse onto, his breathing slowing…to watch him masturbate.

"Won't ask you to put on a show for me," Drew said, his smile ragged.

Good. With the need pooling in his dick and balls, one touch and Elliot would shoot off like a rocket. He yanked his zip down and seized his cock, working himself from root to tip, his hand a furious blur on his flesh.

Drew had one more order. "Eyes on me, Elliot. The whole time. This is for me. Or I'll have you stop—let you get to the edge then tie your hands behind your back and leave you wanting."

His words, their meaning, their weight—their sheer dark promise—hit Elliot like a lash, shooting fire down every nerve ending in his body. Staring into Drew's eyes, seeing their blue shine with renewing heat, he came, cum surging through his punishingly tight fist to spurt from his cockhead between him and Drew…and land on Drew's pants.

Elliot couldn't spare a thought for that, not when he was yelling his agony and ecstasy to the farthest corners of the long, low room, making it echo with his anguish and triumph. Drew's words of praise and admiration, words Elliot could barely hear through the ringing in his ears or catch through the thick white haze clouding his mind, fell on him like a balm over the strokes of his previous command.

When he came to enough to understand where he was and with who, he was in Drew's lap, Drew sitting with his back to a black wood chest, dabbing his face with a soft cloth. A fleecy blanket covered Elliot. Elliot stirred and pulled away a little, to stare up at Drew. "Was that…subspace?" he whispered, not trusting his voice to work as it should.

"No." Drew tucked the blanket around him. "There was a lot of adrenaline and endorphins sloshing around, but it was just a very intense climax, rather than subspace. You mean you've never—?"

Elliot's tight head-shake meant that Drew didn't need to finish asking his question.

"You will. I'll make it my mission," Drew promised, and despite the blanket, Elliot shivered. "Do you keep water or drinks in here?"

"In the other part of the chest from where you got the blanket and cloth," Elliot muttered, feeling cold when Drew set him down and stood. Drew was back almost at once, shaking his head at the sports drink but nevertheless opening it and holding it to Elliot's lips for him, telling him to sip slowly. He unwrapped a protein bar for him and broke pieces off for Elliot to nibble.

"What about you?" Elliot asked him.

"What about me?" Drew leaned back, checking Elliot over.

"You're…" Elliot gestured rather than say *filthy with my spent cum*. "Welcome to have a shower and stay the night."

"I am?" Drew sounded amused.

"I mean, I'd like you to stay the night. With me." Elliot said that to the floor.

Drew didn't challenge him on it, just replied, "I'd like that too."

Now Elliot raised his head to look at Drew, the man who'd given him the sort of sex his soul had craved because it answered a need in him too.

A handsome man, whose looks Elliot liked, and a man whose concern and care were as evident as his wit and humor.

A man who might be the perfect one for him…and who was leaving the country as soon as he'd wrapped up the case he was here to solve.

Trust Elliot to finally work out what he wanted…too late.

Chapter Thirteen

Drew woke suddenly, not sure where he was. Not his apartment, and not Ash's room in the house he shared with friends from work. No, they'd broken up, he remembered, with a mental shrug.

Not the hotel room, with its recycled air and a room freshener smell he never would have chosen. A small snore coming from the pillow next to him had him twisting his head so quickly he almost cricked his neck. *Elliot.* He was here in the man's thankfully neither cute nor cloying bedroom of his something-Victorian house. The man who was smiling in his sleep. Drew bet he had been, too.

A thought struck Drew—he hadn't grabbed his phone as soon as he'd pried his eyes open. Okay, his work circumstances here weren't the same as they were in London, but it wasn't like him. *I'm not here on holiday, for fuck's sake,* he railed at himself. *I've got a fucking international art thief to bring down!* Kislyak was more than that, of course, and the sooner Drew proved that the bastard's corrupt and sick empire was partly funded by the priceless art the crook stole, the better for all concerned. *Well, except Kislyak.*

He eased out of bed, careful not to wake Elliot and, naked, used the bathroom then walked downstairs to find the clothes he'd thrown into the washer-dryer before succumbing to sleep last night. They'd do without being ironed. He took out Elliot's for him, too—both sets had been washed together. Drew's had been just as cum-splattered after that amazing scene.

How much of it had been fueled by the adrenaline of having found the Monet painting? Drew could hardly believe that his hunch had been correct, had paid off to the extent that they'd recovered the artwork and it was right here in this house. Elliot had deserved to get his sub itch scratched after that. No, Drew couldn't pretend the scene had been him indulging Elliot in thanks. Drew didn't even want to pretend, not when it had been as much about him as it had about Elliot.

Speaking—or thinking—of the man, he should prepare him some breakfast. Rifling through cupboards showed him a lack of suitable food but netted him a paper bag from a local bakery, neatly smoothed out for reuse. A quick search on his phone told him the address was a block or so away. He could be back before Elliot woke.

Meeting the neighborhood cat—the huge fluffy ginger beast was too grand to be called a *street* cat—both on his way there and on his return journey delayed him, but he was back, and in the kitchen, when Elliot shuffled in. Listening to the local news on the radio, Drew didn't hear him until his slippers slapped on the tiles.

"Honey oat spelt muffin?" Drew held out the plate. The staff in the bakery had all chorused that out when he'd asked if anyone knew Elliot and, if so, what he usually bought. "Or bacon Cheddar scone? Which I might have exclaimed 'bloody hell!' on seeing and bought immediately. Sorry, I used the back door key and replaced it on the hook." He jerked his chin toward it.

The tea kettle whistled—why didn't people have electric ones?—and he poured the boiling water into the pot.

"I wasn't expecting..." Elliot had wire-framed glasses on his sleepy face.

Drew shrugged. "It's only breakfast. I owe you much more than this. It's—" Something in the news report caught his attention and he snatched up the radio. "What—?"

"The man was found dead, attacked in his own apartment, which was ransacked. It's not known what was stolen, or whether this was gang related, but José Luis Sanchez had a long criminal history..."

"The seller," Elliot gasped, pointing at the radio.

Shit. And shittier—would the guy have had Elliot's phone number, for the police to trace? No, Drew doubted it. Sanchez was the sort to cover his and his clients' tracks as he went. Drew wouldn't let any harm come to Elliot, even though Drew wasn't the only one on the trail of the paintings from the art fair. *Kislyak. Bastard has tentacles everywhere.*

If only Drew were able to use his department's resources and contacts, but he was on his own here. *More like out on a limb.* Yet Elliot had a contact in the local PD. Was there a possibility of utilizing that? Drew would have to be very crafty about it.

An unfamiliar buzzing had Drew freezing, until he worked out it must be Elliot's cell phone, left on a kitchen counter. Elliot seemed just as startled by the sound too. "It's new," he muttered, picking it up and poking at the buttons. "Hello? Oh, hello…" He pointed at the phone, his eyes wide, trying to signal.

Drew took the device and put it on speaker. "*You know this guy?*" he mouthed.

Elliot shrug-nodded. "Yes, I'm interested, as I said. I don't suppose you could bring it to my store?" he asked the caller.

Whoever the man was, he laughed at that. "Unlikely. Meet you at the Pearl seats, out in the open, to have a little talk, huh? Lunchtime?" He rang off.

Drew eyed Elliot. "I get the feeling that's not a respectable fellow art and antiques dealer."

Elliot shook his head. "His name's Silver and he's a fence."

The man was full of surprises. "You know some interesting people."

"I called around, trying to get a lead. Wasn't that right?" Elliot's forehead creased.

"I'd say it was exactly right," Drew replied. He glanced at the kitchen clock. "Shouldn't you be at work by now? And didn't you want to stop by the bank, to drop a little something off at your safe deposit box?"

He packed their breakfast to repurpose as lunch while Elliot, exclaiming in horror, hurled himself up the stairs to shower and dress.

* * * *

He was apologizing to Aldric again an hour later, for all Elliot was the boss. This time wasn't for his unprecedented late arrival with no warning, which had left Aldric worried and dealing with phone calls from the commitments Elliot had blown off. It was for having to slip out almost as soon as he'd gotten there.

"It's been fine," Aldric repeated. "Jonas will be in soon, if we get a rush and I can't handle things."

Is there a rush hour in the antiques trade? Drew had no idea. He caught a puzzled, worried look Aldric didn't disguise well enough when he glanced at him and guessed Aldric was thinking about his boss's tardiness—thinking that it was Drew's fault. The young employee didn't seem to know what to do about it either, his expression switching between happiness that his boss was apparently spending time with someone and picking up on Elliot's guilt and embarrassment at his behavior.

There was nothing Drew could do about it, except try to allay Aldric's suspicions. "My fault," he told the employee. "We lost track of time this morning, and now Elliot's taking me on a walking tour of the area and along the embankment. Oh, you don't call it that here, do you?"

"The Riverwalk." Aldric nodded. "It's pretty."

"We're going to find a good spot for lunch." Drew lifted the canvas satchel he had on one shoulder as proof. *Nothing to see here. Just sightseeing and snacks. Not a meeting with a fence who's handling extremely hot stolen goods.* "All set?" he asked Elliot, once again hating that he was involved to this extent.

Elliot had rushed into his office, murmuring about the half-dozen things he had to see to, and as soon as he'd emerged, gotten caught up attending to a couple who were exclaiming over the bedspread—or so it looked like to Drew—in the window display. Aldric headed to them, joining in and making it clear he could manage. Eventually the string of bells on the shop's door tinkled out Elliot's—reluctant—departure.

"You don't have to keep looking back over your shoulder at the store," Drew said, a little amused. "I know you wouldn't have employed staff who couldn't do their jobs, and do them damn well."

"Oh, thank you." Elliot's cheeks pinkened, just a little, and the lip-lick that accompanied his words had Drew's dick stirring, causing him to shift as he walked.

"I'm sorry about all this," he said, and selfishly feeling the thing he was most sorry about right now was that this wasn't a real stroll through this bustling square and down to the waterfront. He wished he was a real tourist in this vibrant city who'd crossed paths with this man, one who seemed the perfect sub for him, and was enjoying a holiday affair with him. That he'd mentally consigned the case he was here to work on to the back burner staggered him.

"I said I'd help," Elliot replied. He shot Drew a glance out of the corners of his eyes. "And this is…different."

"Different as in out of your routine? Or a complete novelty in the life of an art and antiques trader?" Drew asked.

"As in I like spending time with you." It came out in a rush, as though he'd had to take a deep breath to say it and his honesty humbled Drew.

"I'm really attracted to you too, in case you hadn't picked up on it," he assured Elliot. Elliot admitting to his feelings for Drew was giving Drew a hard-on, something that wasn't convenient when he had to focus. Especially now, with him and Elliot heading down to the walkway that followed the bank of the river. The number of people strolling, and the buzz of the outdoor cafés took him aback.

"Is it livelier than the banks of the Thames?" Elliot asked, watching him react.

"More colorful. I associate one side of the Thames embankment with people hurrying along it to get to work, like I do, and the other's more for tourists. This is a different atmosphere. It seems more for the city to enjoy? It must be fun at night." He pulled his mind from that and back to work. "Let's think how to do this…"

They kept it simple, walking to the open-air seats that Drew guessed also served as an amphitheater, the way the semicircular rows of stone blocks rose from the riverbank as if designed for spectators to watch whatever was on the wooden platform set up over the water. Several people, either individuals or couples or small groups, were sitting chatting on the widely spaced rows, mainly near where trees provided natural shade over the seating.

"You're sure about this?" Drew asked again. Christ, if his bosses knew he was involving a civilian like this. If *Claire* knew! His partner detective sergeant would have a few choice things to say about this. And a few more. Then more still. But it would be nothing Drew wasn't already saying to himself.

With a short nod, Elliot chose the third row up and sat in the middle. Drew selected the one behind him, calculating the width of the gap between each half-moon-shaped row of seating and the next. How long would it take him to spring down to the one below and Elliot? Keeping a sharp eye on him, he was nevertheless aware of two guys making their way along to where he sat, one from the left and one from the right, to sit either side of him.

"You're with him?" one asked, jerking his head to the stone seats below—and Elliot.

Drew nodded. There was no point denying it. The men, lookouts and guards, had no doubt seen him and Elliot arrive.

"Right. We're with him," the guy added.

Him was the man now sitting next to Elliot. Drew had thought the fence's name was Silva, a Hispanic surname, but now guessed it was Silver, his nickname—when he turned his head, sunlight glinted off the mirrored sunglasses he wore. They were oversized, much bigger than a standard military or aviator-style pair.

"I'm going to take my binoculars from my pocket," Drew warned the birddogs, easing the folding compact device free. He got them to his eyes in time to see Silver laying out Polaroid photos on the bench. Each one showed the same picture of a ship. Could it be the Buttersworth he was seeking? Elliot took out his cell phone—Drew had sent him the photos he'd taken in Kislyak's penthouse, so all he had to do was make a comparison, if he couldn't recall the paintings he'd seen on the stall at the fair, but he was hesitating.

Shit. This was taking too long. "I'm going there." Drew stood, leaving them no choice, and was at the seat before they could stop him.

The fence seemed unperturbed by the addition of one extra or even by his men following on the newcomer's heels. "More interest in this item?" he asked.

"May I?" Drew picked up a photograph. *Yes!* He had the artworks he sought memorized, and this was one!

"I couldn't find the pictures you sent me on my damn phone!" Elliot muttered.

"It's okay. What can you tell me about the provenance of this item?" Drew asked, standing protectively behind Elliot.

Silver lowered his glasses a fraction and studied him. He pushed them back in place. "It's stolen. One of the entry-level gang that did the smash and grab at the antiques fair wants me to offload it for them."

His frankness staggered Drew, who was so glad he was recording this meeting, and that Texas was a one-party state when it came to these matters. Could he get Silver to talk, tell him who committed the robbery? Drew doubted it. "I see."

"Do you? Good. So that'll be fifty," Silver said.

"Oh, I have that," Elliot started to reply.

"Thousand," Silver finished.

"*What?*" Elliot burst out.

Silver shrugged. "Interest raises the price." His tone suggested Elliot, as a storekeeper, should know that.

"But I don't have that kind of cash lying around," Elliot protested.

"Not my problem." Silver stood. "You were the first to ask me about those goods, so you get first shot. Bean?"

One of the guys tossed a cell phone to Drew.

"I'm in that. It's a burner, so ditch it after you call me to tell me you got the money. You got until midnight. After that, well, none of your business what happens to the painting after that, is it?"

He stepped away, a guard on either side of him. "Midnight," he called over one shoulder and was gone.

Midnight? Collapsing onto the stone bench beside Elliot, Drew had one thought in his head.

How the hell am I going to get fifty thousand dollars in a few hours?

Chapter Fourteen

"I'm sorry I couldn't convince him to give us more time." Elliot swallowed. He hated to see Drew looking so withdrawn.

Drew stirred. "You have nothing to be sorry about. For what it's worth, you're better at this than some cops I've worked with." He frowned. "*Us* more time? This is my problem. My case."

"For which you still need me...unless you have that amount of money here in the States with you?"

"Not exactly," Drew replied, as Elliot had expected. Fine, Drew definitely did still need him, especially if Elliot came up with some way to get that cash. He was a businessman, a trader—he should be able to think up a way! Damn Silver— *Silver...*

"Silver. Sale," he murmured. "Do you remember white sales, Drew? The original ones, I mean, selling white bedlinen in January, when few people would buy those items, but did when it was steeply discounted? So what if we had not a white but a silver sale? Come on—we have to get back to the store!"

"Elliot!" Drew called after him, but he didn't stop. "Whatever you've got planned, it's not happening!"

He said it again a few more times as they hurried through the Pearl to the store, and Elliot ignored each one.

"Silver," Elliot repeated, rushing inside Intrinsic Value, making the bells tinkle madly and Aldric start. "Ah. Aldric." He needed the coast clear. "Would you mind going to the minimarket for…milk? Drew drinks tea with milk, you see."

"Of course." Aldric blinked in confusion but nodded. "Jonas will be back any second, so I'll go then, when he gets here."

Elliot hadn't factored that in. "No, now is better. Oh, Jonas. Good afternoon."

The latest jingle of bells was the second employee coming in. It struck Elliot that both his assistants looked a little alike, with their dark hair and glasses. Drew had dark hair too. Like Karl. Did Elliot have a type? Most people did. He hoped that if Drew saw any resemblance, he wouldn't think that Elliot…had been intimate with his employees, like he was with Drew.

For the first time, he wondered if the way he'd fallen into bed with Drew—and bent over and kneeled down for him—made Drew think that was the kind of lifestyle he led in general. Maybe it was something they should talk about…if Elliot could bring himself to.

"Jonas, you remember Drew. Jonas, why not accompany Aldric to the market across the square? There's no need to hurry back. It's a lovely day…" Elliot was still babbling when he waved them off, both men looking puzzled, and locked the door behind them.

"And that wasn't at all suspicious," Drew commented. He said nothing more as he watched Elliot adjust the shop window blinds to make it harder to see into the back of the store, then followed him not to his office, but to the small room next to it. "Another safe? If I thought about it, I'd assume you had one on the premises. And we're in here because…?"

"We're having a silver sale." Elliot pulled out a wooden chest, lifted a couple of smaller boxes from inside it and opened them. One fatter box contained a teapot, a taller box a coffee jug and smaller boxes held a cream jug and sugar bowl.

"I'd almost forgotten about this!" he exclaimed, delving into another chest and unearthing a big silver rectangle with handles and compartments. "It's a smoking compendium. Both these pieces are George Vth, as is that complete set of silver flatware over there."

"Elliot." Drew's stern voice stopped him. "You saying what period these items date from is making me wonder—were these your grandparents'?"

He nodded. "There's another trader, Dottie, with a shop, Antique Treasures, out in Boerne. This is the kind of thing she specializes in, and she's been after the tea service since I showed it to her. I'll call her and tell her she can finally buy it, if she does so today."

"Elliot, no. It's very kind of you, but you haven't thought this through." When Elliot's face set in stubborn lines, Drew folded his arms. "I hope you're only doing this so I'll take it out on your hide later, because you can't really think I'd let you go through with getting rid of things that mean a lot? I'm stepping outside to make some phone calls about another way to handle this, so don't do anything until I get back in." He raised a warning finger.

He doesn't understand. But then, how could Elliot expect him to when he barely did himself? Selling these old pieces was right. Elliot preferred books about art or the history of art to psychology, but he'd started reading widely in that area over the last couple of years, trying to understand himself, his psyche and his sexuality. He'd looked into several schools of thought, from mainstream psychology to more fringe beliefs.

In the course of his research, he'd come across theories that suggested holding on to things from the past blocked a person from moving forward, because storage was stagnation. What a person had stored was a dormant energy block, holding the energy from that past period of one's life. What did Elliot stash? Items like these he vaguely recalled being in his grandparents' house, but his memories of his grandparents shouldn't lie in their possessions. He liked to think Gramps and Gran would want him to be happy, to be true to himself, and he was trying.

Of course, he'd started by understanding what made him tick then joining Caress, a club that provided an outlet for those into the Dom–sub sex he craved. He'd even found a pro-Dom there to give the sort of experiences he required for release, even if it was behind closed doors, and in a more controlled, transactional environment. And now…

Now he'd gone from acknowledging his needs to himself to admitting them to a sexual partner and meeting them with him, for God's sake! For most people, that was nothing, but for Elliot it was the equivalent of streaking through Times Square. Okay, so Drew didn't know the whole picture, but…

Elliot locked the safe. Next door in his office, he grabbed his desk phone and dialed Dottie, his determination and energy draining when she was out, and he had to leave a message for her. *Ah.* Maybe he hadn't thought things through in that sense. Was Drew still making phone calls outside? Even if he were having better luck, with the time difference, could he get the money wired in time? How quickly did the British police move? He dropped his head into his hands.

"Elliot?"

Jonas, in Elliot's office doorway, said his name as if repeating it, the expression on his face one of concern. He called over his shoulder to Aldric. "Could you make Drew a cup of tea and take it outside to him…and stay with him for a few minutes, please? I need to talk to Elliot."

"Fine!" Aldric's mutinous tone suggested that it was anything but. His irritated "But I'm tired of being sent away" reached them, as it was meant to.

Jonas entered and closed the door. "Elliot," he began, "We don't have the sort of relationship where we exchange confidences…"

True. Elliot didn't know much about the man he'd hired right after he'd taken Aldric on. Jonas had a strong résumé, with a master's in art history and a first degree in history. He had been a college professor and was again now, teaching some classes at Laurel Heights University, known as the Heights, here in town.

Elliot hadn't asked him why he'd left the university he'd been working at in Dallas or why he'd left lecturing for curating and cataloging, then collecting and selling for Elliot. Jonas was knowledgeable about antiques and his personality made him an asset to Intrinsic Value. That was enough for Elliot. He nodded to show agreement and gestured at a chair on the other side of his desk, for Jonas to sit. Jonas remained standing.

"I'm not prying now but I just went into the safe, and I get the feeling you want to sell the silver items you've been looking at. And, from your manner, sell them quickly. Do you need money in a hurry, Elliot?"

"Yes," Elliot replied.

"I see. Elliot, I don't know what's going on, but I will say that giving in to a blackmailer doesn't work. It might buy time, but in that time a person is so panic-stricken, they can't think or plan clearly and logically."

"What?" Startled by this, Elliot stood. "I'm not being blackmailed!"

"Swear?" demanded Jonas. He came close, his dark-brown eyes looking almost black in their intensity.

"I swear." Elliot breathed out. "I, well, we, Drew and I, need to raise fifty thousand dollars quickly or lose out on an item Drew needs to acquire. We only have a short time to do this. I have no doubt he'll repay me for any outlay I make."

"And it's..." Jonas seemed to be seeking the right word, as if what he was saying were about more than this wish to purchase a piece. "Important?"

"Very much so. To both Elliot and me. To us." He whispered the last part, as if that would make it real.

"Fine." Jonas straightened. "Then...do you have a tuxedo?"

"Do I...?" Elliot goggled.

"And you're free tonight? And we'll need five thousand as a stake." Jonas nodded, his face sharp and decided, and his eyes gleaming like blackcurrants.

Elliot goggled harder.

* * * *

Elliot still didn't think he quite understood when they later pulled into the lot of the Palace Casino out on the northeast loop. And he especially didn't when Jonas checked over both their appearances, then ruffled up his own hair and advised Elliot to do the same.

Jonas's next move was to reach into the back of his car and pull a small bottle of brandy out of a bag. He took a big drink of it, then gargled it before swallowing. "Sorry," he apologized. He blew into his cupped hand and, seeming to decide his breath wasn't right, sloshed a little brandy down the lapel of his tux.

"May I?" Elliot took the bottle and had a nip. He thought he'd need it.

"Have to look the part," Jonas said.

"Jonas..." Elliot handed him the bottle back. "Don't take this the wrong way, but who the hell *are* you?"

Jonas sighed. "Someone who's needed money at various stages of his life. Like, to pay for college—I didn't come from a rich family but knew I wanted to study, then research and teach. And...to pay something else later that threatened to cut me off from that life I'd built. It's...in the past."

But Jonas had left his teaching position at Terrell State University in Dallas. He'd even left the state, relocating to San Antonio. Maybe he'd talk about his past when he was ready, as would Elliot. For now, this had to be enough.

"Let's go do this?" Jonas exited the vehicle. His final act before they headed into the building was to take a slightly battered-looking stuffed rabbit from the bag and clutch it by one ear, swinging it as they walked in. "Yee-hah!" he exclaimed in the lobby, his Dallas accent thick. "I'm feeling lucky! Got my good-luck charm with me—I can't lose!"

He did. Rather a lot, quickly, at roulette, despite trying one wheel after another, his exclamations loud and colorful. "Hell with this. Let's try blackjack?" he called to Elliot, rising and swaying a little as he chose a table, jamming his lucky toy into the seat next to him…which was when he started winning. And continued winning. He bet small amounts at first then larger and larger amounts as the evening went on.

Elliot's heart was thumping like a kettle drum, and he was barely placing bets on the cards as the dealer eased them from the shoe, so he could only imagine how Jonas was feeling. Was he cheating? The management seemed to think so—a hostess came to remove his fluffy rabbit, claiming the seat was needed.

"Hold him for me then!" Jonas demanded, and Elliot noticed a security guard examining the toy.

It didn't seem to affect Jonas' luck or play. Taking the tiniest of sips from the free drinks the casino sent his way, he continued to place bigger bets when high cards were dealt, as if he knew they were coming, and smaller bets when lower cards came out, again, seeming to predict. His chips piled up. The dealers changed twice, the shoe was swapped out for another and different decks of cards were opened, but it made no difference. Jonas was winning big.

"Sir, we wonder if you'd like to take a break, give other casino users a turn at the table?" an employee suggested to Jonas. Two other casino employees were shaking their heads over his furry bunny mascot now.

Jonas stretched and cracked his knuckles. "Reckon I'm about done, anyways." He snagged his toy and went to cash in. Elliot did his best not to gawk at the bundles of bank notes the cashiers stacked into a briefcase. He helped Jonas stagger back to the car, hoping the expression on his face wasn't as wide-eyed as that of the rabbit.

"I have to know!" burst from him before he started the engine. "How did you do that? A hidden camera or, or, microchips in the toy? Or it's blessed and really brings you luck? Aren't you afraid someone will steal it?"

"The rabbit?" Jonas chuckled as he threw it into the backseat. He smoothed his ruffled hair down. "I bought it earlier from a cheap toy store and dirtied it up a little to make it look used. It distracts the casino while I'm counting cards."

"*Counting cards*?" Elliot didn't know whether to laugh or cry.

"It's a skill I cultivated and honed and it's useful for emergencies." Jonas sounded as though he were describing first aid, or map-reading. "As I play the part of an out-of-town tourist, I can only really do it once in each city as word spreads from casino to casino." He patted the case containing over fifty thousand dollars. "So use this wisely."

Elliot doubted that what he needed money for, to buy a stolen painting from a fence, a painting that was a forgery anyway, was wise, but...

Chapter Fifteen

He had the same thought an hour later when he and Drew pulled up at the gates of the rundown business park off the North Interstate 35, where Silver had directed them.

Drew shot him another look. "'A big win at the casino,'" he quoted again. He'd said it a couple of times since Elliot had turned up at his hotel. Together, they'd called Silver to inform him they had the money and been told this address.

Drew shook his head. "I said it before and I'll say it again—for a straitlaced respectable business owner who leads a very orderly, regimented life, you have a lot of hidden sides."

Led a very orderly life. Led. "I told you, I'm trying to, well, live a little. *Live,* really, I suppose." Elliot sought for the words. "I've sheltered behind a routine, behind walls I put up, for a long time."

"Since what happened with your family and you started over," Drew said.

Oh. He had. Elliot gave a nod. "It felt safer." *Then it felt like a straitjacket.* "Then, when I felt ready"—when it chafed to the point of being unbearable—"I started to take steps outside the walls."

Drew laughed. "I think some of the 'steps' you're taking, I, as a cop, should probably have you handcuffed against a wall for."

Elliot coughed. "Did you choose that image deliberately?"

The glint in Drew's eyes said he might have done. It also had Elliot hard. *Handcuffs.* There was something outside of his comfort zone right there. And yes, Drew was an officer of the law…

"Well, for a cop…" It had been occurring to Elliot more and more and he couldn't go any longer without voicing it. "…you're very unconventional." It wasn't that he thought Drew's Metropolitan Police ID was fake, but more that the kind of actions he'd undertaken here in San Antonio didn't seem very orthodox. Drew couldn't imagine Darrell working in the way Drew did, for instance. Darrell's slightly off-the-wall partner, Sean, maybe, but…

"Yeah. The way I'm operating…" Drew blew out a breath. "We'll talk about it later, okay? Focus on this now."

Elliot had to agree that what they had on hand needed all their attention. Drew leaned out and pressed the buzzer at the side of the gate. "Prairie Verbena," he said into the grille, rolling his eyes at Elliot.

"I didn't choose the passphrase," Elliot muttered. He wondered if this was just for them or if Silver tended to use Hill Country wildflowers as passwords. Here on the north side of town, they weren't far from that region.

The gate slid back, and Drew drove them in, past neglected-looking low buildings with flat, corrugated-metal roofs and wide doors. The place seemed deserted, but Elliot wondered what went on behind the doors of each den.

The flat metal door of one building opened slowly, inward, their invitation to park their vehicle and enter. The artificial light inside revealed Silver with more henchman than he'd had earlier, and two of them patted Elliot and Drew down, shaking their heads at Silver to indicate no weapons. They were armed though. Elliot didn't mind admitting to himself that the pools of shadow and circles of metallic light in this large barn-like space were jarring and frightening.

An underling slapped the briefcase on the metal table, the noise ringing, and snapped it open.

"Look at that," Silver gloated. "And you said you couldn't come up with the cash. Amazing what you can do when you're motivated. Tick, Bean..."

His men brought out the painting from what was probably an office off to one side, holding it between them as though they were white-gloved assistants at an auction house, then laid it flat on the table. Drew twitched back the soft cloth covering it, and he and Elliot both stared at the picture of the clipper. It was dramatic and yet graceful, and the wealth of detail made it seem like a photograph. It was the painting Drew sought.

"Thank you," he said at last to the seller.

"Oh, you're welcome." Silver closed the briefcase with a snick. "You can have the cloth too. You know..." His tone was casual, but Elliot would have preferred to grab what they'd come for and run. "I been looking up this painter, and these works..."

"Oh?" Elliot tried not to stare too obviously at the door.

"They're not that valuable."

"The man who wants it really wants it." Elliot tried a shrug.

"And the gang who did the raid are really sorry they did it," Silver added. In the silence that followed he looked from one to the other. "Are you gonna ask why?"

"Why?" Elliot felt he had no choice but to play along.

"Because someone big is after them. Well, after what they stole, but same thing really. Yeah, someone dangerous. Someone you don't want to cross."

Images of things that had happened so far flickered through Elliot's mind. The stallholder. Sanchez, the petty thief.

"Well, I don't want to cross him," Silver continued. "So I'm clearing out, see?"

Elliot realized what he meant, that there was nothing *to* see. Whatever this place had been used for, it was empty now. "Thank you," he replied, not knowing what else to say. This whole interaction was so far removed from his normal reality that it felt surreal.

"Can you tell us anything about this guy?" Drew broke in.

Silver inclined his head at him. "It'll cost ya."

"Well, I'm a little broke." Drew scowled at the briefcase. "Can I owe you?"

Silver sucked in air through his teeth. "Owing me ain't wise." One of his men laughed. "But I'll give ya a freebie. He's one of you." He shot a glance at Drew.

A cop? Was that what he meant? A chill rippled along Elliot's spine. "Drew—"

"British." Drew cut Elliot off.

"English, European, whatever." Silver's shrug said it was all the same. "And one of *you*."

This time his gaze took in both of them. Elliot flushed.

"Hey, don't bother me. Leaves more women for us," Sliver assured them, to more chuckles from his posse. "But I heard he's hardcore. In all senses. Likes to play…hard and extreme."

"Like BDSM?" Drew asked.

"Maybe. But maybe not that sane or safe. Consensual, I dunno." His tone suggested he did and that the answer was no.

Elliot tried to puzzle through Silver's words. So this guy, this crook, was into risky play?

"Well, enjoy. Don't look for me for a while as I'll be out of town until this is all over. Give us five minutes to get clear before you leave, understood?" With a final smirk, Silver sauntered out, fifty thousand dollars richer than he'd been when he walked in.

"Examine the painting right away," Elliot suggested, and they hurried back to Drew's car and the tools he'd stashed in it.

Drew eased away the frame in one corner, as he'd done before, peeling away the picture placed on top of the original, to disguise it. Even in the light of the dashboard, the saturated hues and fragmented blocks of color made Elliot gasp, "A Cezanne."

"*Sunrise at Châteaufort*." Drew levered the fake painting down again, covering the priceless work. His face shone with elation when he looked up. "That's two of the paintings recovered. Two links back to Kislyak."

"But you need to get the third? You can't go back to London with just two?"

"I'm not sure." Drew's attention was on his task of covering the painting carefully. "The case is complicated. It's ongoing and evolving."

Well, that's me told. Elliot bit his bottom lip. "We have to get this into a safe as soon as possible," he said.

Drew started the car. "I don't like it being on your property even for one night. We'll go straight to the safe deposit box first thing tomorrow."

They'd been driving a few minutes when Elliot noticed the stiffening of Drew's shoulders and neck as he glanced more and more into the driving mirror, and the tightening of his hands on the wheel of the Camry. The headlights of a car behind them shining brightly into their vehicle gave him a clue as to why. "The car behind…it's too close."

"And been so for a few minutes and getting closer." Drew sped up a little…and the black Escalade's speed increased in tandem. Only much more so, until it was almost tailgating them.

"Maybe they want to pass?" Elliot asked.

Drew flashed the Camry's lights then waved his hand out of the window in a *pass, you moron* gesture. The car didn't, just inched closer, so Drew had to speed up to avoid getting bumped, then gripped the wheel hard to take a bend at the high speed. "*Shit,*" he breathed.

The Escalade loomed black and impenetrable as a shark. Elliot could no longer pretend he thought it was some innocent road user who happened to be going their way, objecting to their speed and yet unable to overtake them on the road. That this was happening if not in broad daylight but out in the open, and almost casually like this, with no squeals of tires of screeches of brakes, or bangs and thuds, seemed strange and wrong.

"Hang on," Drew ordered, and Elliot grabbed for the roof bar above his door just as the Escalade bumped them, shoving them forward a foot. The shock as much as the actual thud jolted him. He nodded an *I'm fine* at Drew's glance across at him.

The speed Drew was driving pinned him to his seat, like he was on a ride at the fair, and he couldn't hold in a cry as the Camry almost fishtailed when Drew took a bend too fast. Drew wrestled with the wheel to get the vehicle under control, wrenching hard to avoid a small pickup truck coming the other way. Did they clip it?

"Up ahead." Drew gave a quick chin jerk at the windshield. "See what I do?"

"Another black Escalade?"

"Think they want to box us in. Really hang on." Drew gave an almighty swerve, forcing the car into a half-circle and into the lane going the other way, back the way they'd come. There wasn't much traffic but enough for drivers to send up a chorus of blasts on the horn and curses…and some cheers.

"Do you think they saw us leave Silver's? Have they been tailing us?" Elliot exclaimed.

"Let's not wait to find out." Drew pulled off at the first exit and took one B-road after another, driving in circles and figures of eights to reach the underground parking lot of Drew's hotel until Elliot was lost and disorientated.

His hand shook when he tried to open his door and get out.

"Hey. Take your time," Drew advised. "It's okay to be scared."

"I am," Elliot admitted. He might have wanted to step outside his routine, make himself leave his comfort zone, but he hadn't reckoned on any of this. "Drew, I know you've been working this alone, but maybe it's time to call your bosses in on this case now."

"Yeah, about that."

Elliot knew he didn't want to hear what Drew looked reluctant to say, but he had to.

"I'm working alone because I'm working unofficially. I got suspended from duty for going after Kysliak." Drew's lips flattened into a line. "So I have to see this through and nail the bastard or I'm out of a job…which will be the least of my problems if I've taken a shot at the king and missed, as my partner pointed out to me. I'm sorry I didn't tell you, but I'm on my own with this."

Elliot was glad he was sitting, because now he knew what it felt like to have the rug pulled from under him—if he'd been on his feet, he would have crashed to the floor. "So you lied to me. Again. Just like you did at first, not revealing you were a cop investigating an incident I was a witness to. You remember, when I thought you wanted to meet me for me, not because of needing something for your job."

"Elliot." Drew's voice went a little way toward calming him. "You can't be in any doubt how much I enjoy seeing you. Spending time with you. We have something real and hot between us."

He thought so. He *hoped* so. "So give it a chance. Give us a chance, Drew. Let's really spend some time together, without all this."

"This? How?" Drew looked wary.

"Hand this over. All of it. Your investigation, the paintings, everything. To Scotland Yard or the SAPD.

Hell, Interpol. Any official body who can take it over. It's the sensible, safe thing to do, anyway. And you'd be free here in the city—"

"Hand it over? I can't do that." Drew looked scandalized. "I have to see this through. You know that."

"I know *you* think that. Well, I'll leave you to it, then. I'm sure you can stash this in the hotel safe for the night, and I'll notify the bank that you'll be there first thing to use my safe deposit vault."

"Elliot." Drew caught his hand. "I meant what I said. We have something special."

"I..." Elliot sighed. "I'm not in the right frame of mind to discuss this now...but I want to believe it." Oh, how he did. "Could we meet for lunch tomorrow? I've shown you I'm prepared to invest in a relationship, in us, and I want to see you're going to do the same."

Chapter Sixteen

Who the hell does Elliot Douglas think he is? Drew scowled again, exasperated that Elliot's handsome face, with his big tawny eyes and silvering hair, kept getting between him and the case notes he was updating the next morning. Not the morning after, sadly, following Elliot flouncing off to his car and his own bed.

For a guy with such submissive tendencies, Elliot was a pushy bastard. *Oh, why did I have to think of those submissive tendencies?* Drew groaned and shifted on the chair at his desk, then turned the chair itself so he didn't catch a glimpse of the other seat, the armchair where Elliot had kneeled to take a spanking. His cheeks had colored so well, and God, that ass of his, so tight and hot.

Drew didn't know what he'd loved reaming the most, Elliot Douglas' sweet ass or his even sweeter mouth. Elliot had taken a skull fucking better than any other partner Drew had ever played with, even the twinks who wore eyeliner and mascara, so it ran down their faces as tears trailed from their eyes. Although, mascara would make Elliot's yellowy-brown eyes pop. *But then the cute gold tips to his eyelashes would be lost.*

Drew checked himself. He hadn't realized he'd studied Elliot's face in that much detail when they'd eaten supper in this room, or lunch at the place near Elliot's store…or when they'd shared Elliot's bed. He'd been hoping they'd sleep together last night too, after another round of sex…possibly with Drew taking his leather belt to Elliot's toned, responsive ass cheeks.

Shit! He had to concentrate. He normally had no trouble focusing on work and pushing everything, relationship included, to the back of his mind. To the deepest recesses of his mind, he supposed Ash and most of his exes would say. This, this cocktail of emotions swirling in him—longing, regret, hope—distracting him from his work, showed why relationships were not compatible with work. And he had to work. Had to solve this or— Well, career-wise and maybe every other-wise, there was no 'or'.

He dragged his pen down the chain of evidence he'd documented that connected Kislyak to the paintings. That was one thing and the chain of custody the other. He'd taken charge of the evidence—the priceless evidence—and had chronologically documented its retrieval, being careful to record and photograph every stage, even that of placing it in the bank deposit, but was well aware that the latter, being outside the remit of law enforcement, might not withstand a legal challenge.

The case needed more than just the retrieval of all three paintings to prove that these were the same ones Kislyak had flaunted in his penthouse and that Drew had photographed there. It also required more than the man having been in the same city at the time the works of art had been stolen to prove that he'd been involved. Would recovering the third painting strengthen Drew's case?

He studied a photocopy of it, Sisley's *Wheatfield near Ponthierry,* then the photograph he'd taken of the painting he was sure was being used to cover it, a softer, hazier landscape awash in shades of blue. How could he find that?

The ringing of the room's phone had Drew groping for the receiver. Still buried in his thoughts as he was, it took him a few seconds to place the voice and the name. Patrol Officer Darrell Williams was the partner of the younger assistant at the antiques store, wasn't he? When Drew understood why the guy was calling him, he sat bolt upright in his chair, his hands clutching his research notes.

"Sorry, please tell me again?" he begged Darrell.

"The local accent's hard to understand, right?" Darrell gave a quick laugh. "Let me repeat—the paintings you said you were at that arts fair looking for, the ones that were stolen when the stall was robbed? We think we got one of 'em."

"Really?"

"Well, we're not sure. So I was wondering if you could come into the station, see if you can identify it? And authenticate it? Is that the word?"

"Of course." Drew's heart thumped hard. "I'd be glad to." He strained to hear something muffled in the background. "Make sure I'm not charging for the consult?" he repeated bemused.

"Excuse my partner." Darrell's voice sounded exasperated. "Officer O'Hara's…"

Drew supplied the rest of the sentence for himself. He'd worked with funny-guy types too. "I'd be pleased to come and provide whatever help I can," he assured the policeman, gathering his research together as he spoke. His phone dinged—a message from Elliot. Well, no time now. "My pleasure." *And an answer to a prayer that I hadn't quite gotten around to making.* "Give me the address?"

* * * *

It was Patrol Officer O'Hara who came into the reception of the police substation to meet Drew. With his rusty-red hair and wiry build, he looked so like some of the guys Drew worked with in London that he felt almost homesick for a moment.

"You're Officer Williams' partner?" he asked, shaking hands. "I think I heard your voice on the phone earlier."

Officer O'Hara eyed him up and down. Drew had dressed a little flamboyantly, donning a brightly patterned vest and even a tie, wanting to look as if he belonged in the art world and had nothing to do with law enforcement.

"Call me Drew," Drew instructed.

O'Hara spluttered. "Because you're an artist? Geddit? Draw, drew?"

Drew laughed. "As in Andrew."

"Oh." The man seemed disappointed. Maybe he thought everyone involved with art had a tag, like graffiti artists did. "I'm Sean."

Drew resisted making any of the quips he wanted to at this statement, merely casting a long glance at Sean's luxuriously thick and visibly unshorn hair. "How did you acquire the piece?" he asked as Sean led him along a corridor.

"The gun?" Sean put a protective hand on his Glock. "It's standard issue. Oh yeah, cops aren't armed in London, right?"

"Sorry, I meant the piece of art," Drew clarified. "And no, they're not as a rule, but each force does have a firearms unit on call."

"Unbelievable." Sean whistled through his teeth. "Hey, Laurie," he said to a fellow officer who passed them. "You know cops in England don't carry guns?"

She rolled her eyes and continued with her duties.

"The painting?" Drew prompted.

"Oh yeah. In here." Sean nodded at the officer inside the evidence room. "Right here, in fact." It lay on a table, not far from the door.

"You're just logging it in now." Drew understood. "May I?" He helped himself to disposable gloves from a box and donned them, keeping his face expressionless and his breathing steady…even when he pulled open the mouth of the big drawstring bag someone had put the painting into.

"Could you…?" he asked Sean and tried not to flinch when Sean grabbed the end of the bag and yanked it free of the object it held.

The metallic gray and fluorescent white light of the crowded, chaotic room did the painting no favors, but Drew had never seen such a luminous sight—not the muted serenity of the body of water that met the gentle sky, but what he knew must be underneath. He compared it to the photo on his phone just to double check, but he knew.

"It's the same Alfred Thompson Bricher I saw at the antiques fair, yes," he confirmed. "I can't say if it's authentic without doing some tests…?" If they left him alone with the painting…

"Thanks." Sean scribbled in his notebook. "Not at this stage, I guess. I'll check."

"You know, this could be a rare early work and so *extremely* valuable," Drew invented. "You'll make sure to keep it firmly under lock and key and keep a strict track of it, won't you?"

"Can do. Marv, stash it in the back with those keys of coke?" Sean ordered the other office behind the desk.

Drew's phone rang and he silenced it with an apologetic grimace. Elliot again. "So you caught the gang who raided the fair?" Drew asked, sounding as casual as he could.

"Not exactly. The leader, if you can call him that, Ramon Wells, perp known for these smash and grabs, like on ATMs? He came in with that this morning!" Sean gave a chuckle. "I know, right? Just waltzed in and gave himself up. And asks if we can keep him in—says he'll be safer in custody!"

"*Safer?*" Drew prompted.

"Than he is at large with these goods after stealing them. Said he heard it was the kiss of death or something." Sean looked a little nervous now. "I guess he means it's cursed, right? I hate all that stuff."

"Well, the art world is superstitious." Drew thought fast. Kiss of death—could that be a reference to Kislyak? He'd thought that before—the phrase had come up when a trail went cold. "Oh, but he means it as a nickname, doesn't he? At least, I've heard it, for that famous art dealer. Kis-something. Rich guy. Business owner."

"*Kislyak*? Roman Kislyak?" Sean took the bait. "I know the name. Who doesn't?"

"As I said, he's an art dealer to the rich."

"*He's* rich. Owns business all over, yeah? Including in the States. In this state, even. Think he has property here too."

"Oh, the super-rich do that, have houses in places they visit. Saves booking a hotel, I suppose." Drew willed Sean to spill more. "What businesses does he have here?"

"Nothing like an art gallery, if that's what you're thinking. Nothing concrete, either. But the rumors that fly around that guy…" Sean took a look up and down, but no one was listening. "I remember, a few years back, it was said he had his fingers in a lot of tacos in Austin. They even said he was 'in business' with Yuriy—you heard of him in England? Real crook. Nasty. Boss type—you know what I mean, right?—but a has-been now. Like, Yuriy used to run things for him?"

"Organized crime?" Drew's heart rate picked up the pace. "Racketeering? RICO stuff?"

"I guess." Sean gave him rather a surprised look. "'Course, could be all talk. Yuriy's an old man who hangs out in a rundown bowling alley now, talking of his glory days, you know? Well, thanks."

"Yes, don't let me keep you." Drew beat the hastiest retreat he could, because he was going to Austin, following up on the garrulous Sean's information. In his car, an internet search into bowling alleys in that city showed him a very high number. Adding Yuriy's name to his search terms got him an article with a picture of a winning bowling team posing with a trophy. The team, Bowl U Over, were based at Yuriy's lanes, Big Bowling.

He noticed Elliot had called again. This time, Drew replied.

Sorry – got a lead and checking it out. Might be my one shot at getting close to the target. Back later.

He had to do this, didn't he?

An hour and a half later, Drew was on the outskirts of Austin, heading for what he could easily see wasn't the best part of the city. Big Bowling, when he found it, fitted the area. The outside was shabby, and its orange plastic and faded wood interior décor spoke of a heyday long gone. *Big and empty bowling,* Drew thought, seeing how few lanes were in use and how many of the lights on the low ceiling flickered.

An air of sad neglect hung over the place. A case on the wall, just inside the doors, held the same trophy he'd seen in the article, and not many others. He walked down the aisle between the rows of seats to the score tables near the lanes. "Hey, man," he called to a guy wiping down the far one. "Yuriy about?"

"In the back." The kid flicked his cloth toward a small door between the final lane and the wall. He didn't look as though he were running security or would ask Drew his business.

Drew gave him a nod of thanks as he passed. The door was marked 'Private' so he knocked before he shoved it open—to see a man exiting via the fire door on the opposite side of the small room.

"Yuriy?" Drew called, hurling himself across the cluttered, crowded office. "I want to talk to you!"

The man was in his late fifties and limped, so Drew didn't have him to chase him very far through the parking lot before he was on him. "Police!" Drew said. "So I wouldn't go for your gun, if I were you. Turn around slowly."

When the overweight man did, Drew held out his Metropolitan Police badge.

"'S that? Like Interpol?" Yuriy wheezed, peering at it.

Drew gave a sort of nod, sort of shrug. "Relax. I don't want you. Just information on your business partner, Kislyak." He almost staggered under the curses raining from Yuriy at the name and switched on his recording device.

"Ex-partner, I take it?" Drew tried, leading the man inside.

"I cut him in on my empire, and the bastard took over and cut me out. Cut *me* the fuck up too." Yuriy rubbed his leg, stretching it out as he sat.

"Business can be tough," Drew agreed, wanting to leap in elation at what he was finding out. He'd suspected all this and more. "What was it, different ideas on expansion versus consolidation?"

Yuriy scowled. "So I was skimming a little off the top. He didn't need it!"

"Talk me through the business. Your empire. How you built it, what happened…" Drew invited.

It made bleak listening, not just the illegality of the guy's acquisitions and holdings, but how Kislyak had encouraged him to ditch his long-standing crew and partners, including his wife and her family, to go in with him and his ideas, then dumped him once he'd established himself.

"I got nothing," Yuriy finished. "Spent my life working, building, and got nothing. Because of getting near that vicious bastard. He don't even need all this!" He gestured around. "He just likes it. Likes somewhere to play. Enjoys that."

"Enjoys…?" Drew queried, thinking of what he'd sensed about the thug. That coiled, misdirected energy.

"The enforcement. He's into some weird shit. Those hardcore clubs? He's a member of all the extreme ones. Likes to play hard, wherever he is. Filth."

Drew agreed, even if for different reasons. "I was never here," he said, getting up to go.

With a bitter "Yeah? Fucking wish I wasn't," Yuriy flipped him the bird.

There'd be no point asking him to go on the record, even if Drew had the authority to. Which he didn't, because he was pursuing this, well, illegally. The parallel with the man he'd come to interview struck him hard. A guy who'd lost everything because of getting close to Kislyak.

Drew sat in his car, looking around the ruins of all Yuriy had worked for and hoped for and thought *shit*. Had he done that? Destroyed whatever chance he had with Elliot? He picked up his phone—the message Elliot had sent after Drew had missed lunch would suggest so.

Normally Drew would have shrugged at a guy not fitting into his life. *What life? You mean work.* Like *Yuriy*. He gave a hollow laugh. But there was more. Or should be. Elliot was taking steps to have one—couldn't Drew be brave enough to do the same? Elliot had been patient and given him a change after learning Drew wanted him for his connections and the help he could provide for the case. *He gave us a chance.*

And Drew wanted that. Wanted Elliot. Wanted a relationship. Which meant he had to work for it—if it wasn't too late, or he'd be left obsessed and bitter…and alone.

Chapter Seventeen

Elliot not only opened the door to him but did so in his bathrobe, looking so soft and fluffy in the white toweling that Drew's heart leaped. But when Elliot folded his arms and put up a wall like the ones he'd been trying to come out from behind, everything in Drew plummeted.

"A little late for lunch, aren't you?" Elliot remarked and the echo of Claire wondering why Drew was giving her lunch at almost dinner time served to remind him of *his* patterns and behavior too. Well, if Elliot could re-educate himself…

"I'm so sorry." Drew held up his hands in apology.

"And that's all you've got to say." Elliot took a step back, preparing to go inside.

"No. I have a lot to say." *But where to start?* "Mainly that you were right—I live for work and everything else comes second. And I wish I'd met you today to talk about things. But I did it again, went off chasing after a lead. If you're still mad at me, I don't blame you. My life is either work or compartmentalized sex as stress relief second to that. It's not about feeling or exploring, and it should be, with you. I want it to be, with you. If you'll give me a chance to try."

"So this is the big romantic declaration?" Elliot glanced pointedly at Drew's hands that were empty of candy or chocolates.

"It's the declaration of intent. Not so much chocolates and flowers as my heart on the line. On the starting line, actually—I want to *start* a *relationship* with you." Yep, in the grand scheme of extravagant gestures and shout-it-from-the-rooftops announcements, it was hardly world-shattering, but...

"Oh." Elliot blinked. Did he realize how this was as big a step for Drew as some of the ones he'd taken? "But what about the case? Kislyak?"

Despite the tension, Drew wanted to smile at how Elliot *got* him. "I found out more stuff today. The third painting's in the SAPD, for one thing. You were right about another thing, that it's time to bow out. To hand this over. But can we not talk about that now?"

"Really?" Elliot looked pleased but wary. "So what do you want to talk about?"

"I don't really want to talk. What I'd like to do is be invited in, to start our relationship off properly by making love to you." Drew gave him a crooked grin.

"Make..." Elliot almost squeaked but stepped aside to allow Drew entrance.

Drew pulled him into his arms and held him tight. "Yeah," he said in Elliot's ear, which he nipped, to make Elliot shudder. "Would you like that?" Elliot stirred a little and hesitated. Drew understood. "Oh, you thought I meant some bland, vanilla lovemaking?" He bit down a little harder on Elliot's lobe and moved to look him in the face. "I know you crave it spicy…which suits me. I'll give you all the spice you can handle, then a little more."

He loved how his words had Elliot huge-eyed and breathing fast. He slid his hands to the back of Elliot's head, spearing his fingers into his temples and thrusting his tongue into his mouth. Elliot clung to him and kissed him just as fiercely, making Drew hard.

He pulled away. "I want you to go on up first and get some toys ready for us to play with. Okay?" At Elliot's nod, Drew turned him around and swatted his ass to get him moving. He gave Elliot thirty seconds, then followed him into his bedroom.

"Still go, slow and stop and knocking your hands or feet twice?" Drew asked.

Elliot nodded.

"Good. Come here." Drew stripped the gown from him. Elliot fresh from the shower smelled delicious and his cock was already standing tall, inviting Drew to make it glisten. Elliot was thick and his shaft had an intriguing curve to it that Drew intended to get to know with his tongue.

"Can I undress you?" Elliot asked, making Drew recall he hadn't really been naked in front of Elliot yet. He'd pulled his clothes off when Elliot was half asleep, but…

"Yes. And next time you can explore me," Drew promised, helping Elliot remove his clothes. Elliot's hands on him made each patch of skin sensitized, as though Elliot were tonguing each centimeter. It reminded Drew that something he enjoyed was sitting at his ease while a sub at his feet licked and sucked his balls. The image of Elliot with his nose deep in Drew's pubic hair as he took Drew's sac into his hot mouth almost had his erect cock spurting.

He backed Elliot to the bed, kissing him again, then gave him a gentle push onto the mattress and turned him onto his front. "Going to be good and take everything I give you?" he whispered in Elliot's ear. "Or be a brat and force me to give you more? I'm good either way…and I bet you will be too."

Elliot hesitated, and Drew wanted to smile at the sub weighing up his options. "Both," he said finally, making Drew smile into the nape of his neck.

Drew nudged Elliot's legs apart with one knee and sat between them to get a good look at Elliot. "You're so hot," he said. He leaned over him, pressing his groin into Elliot's ass as if testing their fit—not that there was any need. Drew knew how well they fit together. "Let me see you?"

He gave Elliot no time to refuse or even ask what he meant, instead moving Elliot's bent leg up higher to spread his ass cheeks and part them. "Beautiful," Drew told him. Elliot shivered, and Drew gave him a moment to get used to that position, using the time to snag a pillow and ease it under Elliot's hips then angle the bedside lamp so it cast light on Elliot's hole and threw bars of shadow down his spine.

Drew used the trails as a guide to kiss down, right to the base, loving how Elliot clutched his fingers tightly into the sheet below him when Drew reached the top of his cleft. "Make all the noise you like," Drew invited, going onto his knees to lick down Elliot's crease. Beneath him, Elliot whimpered.

Drew pulled Elliot's cheeks apart and nosed his hole, then kissed it. Although he'd showered and that sandalwood scent clung to him, Elliot smelled musky and raw there, and Drew liked that better. He licked over Elliot's pucker, a long, slow swipe at first, then again, a little rougher and quicker, curious how Elliot would react.

Elliot's breath caught and he let out a gasp, but the best was his muscles fluttering under Drew's tongue when he traced its tip in a tight circle around Elliot's hole, testing and seeking. "Oh, you like this," Drew surmised.

If the noise Elliot made wasn't him begging for more, the undulation of his body beneath Drew was. Drew had to tighten his grip on Elliot's cheeks and, when he shifted his thumbs, deep white indents showed. Drew widened Elliot's legs farther until he must have been feeling the stretch and burn...and very exposed. "Okay?" Drew asked, blowing gently onto the wetness.

The *yes* Elliot gave in answer became a long hiss due to Drew pressing his tongue into Elliot at the same time as he rubbed his thumbs along the outside of his rim. Elliot cried out and froze, as if shocked, but then his hips rocked and the cry turned pleading—he wanted more.

"But do you deserve more?" Drew asked.

"*Yes!*" Elliot shouted, arching his butt into Drew's face.

"Sure?" Drew queried, sadistically, and before Elliot could answer, gave it to him, forcing his tongue deep inside Elliot's channel to fuck him with it. It only took half a minute until Elliot's hole was softened and dripping wet, and Drew he could slip a thumb in beside his tongue easily.

Drew raised his head. "I wish you could see how fucking slutty you look," he murmured. "Next time we'll film this." How would Elliot react to the sight Drew was almost climaxing at now, the string of saliva dripping from Drew's mouth to Elliot's hole and trickling down to his balls?

Drew sat back, working Elliot open with his thumb and forefinger, using saliva for lubrication, rather than stop and grab the lube, for all Elliot had left it on the bed. He liked the slightly rough clutch of Elliot's passage like this, without the extra silky glide the lube added.

"Yeah, I wish you could see what I see, you taking this. We're definitely videoing this. Now, you do know I'm going to rim until you're begging me to let you come? And Elliot, you're so sensitive—you'll be begging hard."

Elliot grinding his hips into the pillow, trying to get friction on his aching cock, earned him a ringing slap on one butt cheek. Drew eased his hips back…so he could push his tongue in farther and at the same time, half roll Elliot over to get a hand under him. He used it to grip the base of Elliot's dick, ringing it tightly to stop him coming. Elliot was thrashing too much for Drew to continue eating him out, making him stop. "Should have put you in a cock ring," he mused. "Well, it's not too late. And next time I'm strapping you down. Or up—on a St. Andrew's cross."

Elliot did the freeze then thrust thing again, meaning he was considering it…and liked the idea. Which reminded Drew that he'd promised Elliot playtime with toys. "I know you want my dick spearing into you and stuffing you, but all in good time," he said huskily, sliding free of Elliot. He glanced over at the toys Elliot had waiting and his lips curled.

"We can do better than that," he said and leaned back to open the top drawer of Elliot's nightstand, where he did a double-take at the anal beads. No tiny spheres on a string, this was a twelve-inch row of black silicone bumps with no gaps in between, growing in size from the smallest at the tip to the fattest, largest end bead before the stopper. Even the handle looked massive…which would make grasping and wielding them easy…and pleasurable.

"Look, Elliot." Drew made sure Elliot saw him take them. "Now why do I think you left these right at the front of your drawer, where they'd be easily found? Oh yes, because you're a pushy sub." He appreciated how wide Elliot's eyes grew when Drew gripped the handle and slapped the beads against the palm of his other hand and how Elliot jumped at the meaty *thwack*.

Drew squirted lube onto his palm to slick the toy up, taking care to coat the last, thickest bead and that Elliot watched him do it. He understood Elliot more now—anticipation and nervousness were a big part of things for him. "No talking now. No noise," he ordered. Elliot would find *that* hard.

He said nothing either as he bent and gave the tiniest rub of the toy at Elliot's exposed asshole then penetrated him with the tip, sliding the first bead halfway inside.

Elliot gasped. "Sorry," burst from him.

"You're not sorry," Drew surmised. "Not by the way you're trying to push yourself back, to take more into that greedy hole of yours." Judging Elliot's body heat had spread the lube and his passage was slick enough, he gave Elliot what he wanted and pushed the silicone bead fully in. The gargled noise he heard was Elliot smothering his groan with his hand over his mouth.

"Have you taken these before?" Drew asked, and Elliot nodded. "But not the whole length." Elliot shook his head. "Well, you are now. Next one…" The third bead was about five centimeters in circumference he assessed, and it stretched Elliot's rim wide. Drew left it in the hole for long seconds before using the handle to push it in.

"You can take it." Drew rubbed his back. "I'm proud of you. You should be proud of yourself. I don't mean just of what your body can physically take…like the last one." He used the toy's handle to roll the beads in and out, just slightly, but the loud moan Elliot gave told Drew he'd stroked over the bump of Elliot's prostate.

"I said no noise!" Drew roared and slapped Elliot's cheek…to make the beads rub over his gland again. This had Elliot burying his face in the sheets under him to absorb the sounds he let loose. "I like prostate play." Drew kept his tone light. "Internal"—he pulled the toy so the bead that he'd just inserted popped out again…for Drew to thrust back in—"and external."

He gave Elliot a second to figure that out before he rubbed Elliot's taint, hoping to stimulate the gland from the outside. He didn't need to—the beads were doing all the work—but, well. "Final one," he said, preparing Elliot.

"No. Please. I can't," came from Elliot in a feeble gasp.

Drew listened to his words…and the word he didn't say—his safe word. He didn't give any signal either. "Oh, I think you can," he replied, "So you're going to." Elliot might not want to, but he needed to. "It's wide and should stretch you, which is good because I'm going to fuck you after you've come."

He had to, or climax over Elliot's ass. He almost was. The final bead of the toy looked obscenely big and fat. Drew judged it as being about seven and a half centimeters round. He kept his grip firm on both the handle of the beads and, reaching around, Elliot's cock. As he'd expected, Elliot was almost coming. Without warning, he slid the final bump in, so the row was buried up to its hilt.

Elliot hollered, and all it took was Drew pulling the toy free with one hand and stroking his other up Elliot's dick and thumb his slit to make him scream—and come in a huge wave, jetting over Drew's hand. His climax was one of the longest Drew had ever seen, pulse after pulse, spasm after spasm, and he spooned Elliot, bending over his curled-into-itself body to ride the waves with him.

"You look so hot...you're doing great," Drew murmured, waiting for Elliot to come back to himself. Pressed so close to him, he felt Elliot's hole flexing around emptiness, and he chuckled into Elliot's damp neck. "Good thing you want more, because remember what I promised?" He didn't know how he'd managed to keep from coming, but he had. "I said I was going to fuck you, and I am. Now."

Chapter Eighteen

Elliot, still panting, red and sweaty, stared at Drew. It was what they'd discussed, Drew forcing Elliot further and further out of his safe zone each time. Sex with a hook-up he'd had one drink with in a bar hadn't been that big a step, but SM sex, Elliot getting his ass spanked hard then fucked harder? *That was a giant step.* And their next scene, Drew holding Elliot's head so he could fuck his throat?

Forcing me to deep throat him, to take his cock until I choked. Then swallow him, then take the rest to the face? Elliot still shivered at the memory of that, and Drew watching him jerk off after. *And now this?*

He'd bought that toy, fantasizing about its girth, and had used it a little, getting as far as the third bump in solo play. And now he'd taken the entire thing! His ass ached and he squirmed at the memory, recalling Drew's words that he should be proud of himself and not just for what his body could take.

Drew was casting a quick look around the room then back at Elliot. As if reaching a decision, he moved the armchair more fully into the bay window…and opened the drapes. The window faced the street. It was unlikely anyone would be standing outside, peering in, or even looking from a neighboring window, but the public exposure of it stole Elliot's breath.

And Drew seemed to know it, going by the smirk on his face. When he sat in the big padded chair, his cock stood up proudly. He gestured at the condoms on the bed. "Cover me."

"I…"

"Heard me. Now."

Barely able to walk, Elliot approached with the condom and, fingers shaking, opened the packet and rolled the latex onto Drew's cock. "I didn't bring the lube." Elliot turned to go back to the bed but Drew's grip on his arm stopped him.

"It's lubricated and so are you. You had plenty of prep, so hop on up."

Still not believing he was doing it, Elliot did, climbing to straddle Drew. Even after taking that toy to his ass, he thought Drew looked huge, sitting there, giving a lazy pull to his dick. Elliot tried to sink down on it, but his sweat-dewed body slipped, and he missed. Drew grabbed his face.

"You'd better not be stalling."

Elliot gave the tiniest head-shake, all he could manage, and this time held Drew's cock steady as he lowered over him again. He grunted when the head breached him, making sensitive tissues sting, and Drew's hand round the back of his neck brought his mouth to Drew's. Drew opened Elliot's lips with his and took his agonized cry into his own lungs, sharing Elliot's reaction to the penetration with him. It was shockingly intimate.

Elliot's hands flew out and landed on Drew's shoulders. He pulled his head away a little to suck in a breath—Drew was pulsing in his ass in a way that a plug or beads or a dildo never could, warm and alive, and he moaned at the feel.

"You can take me," Drew told him.

He moved a hand to Elliot's pec, and Elliot didn't understand why, until Drew closed his finger and thumb around Elliot's nipple and squeezed. Again, Drew swallowed Elliot's gasp.

"And I want to see you take this," Drew added, increasing the squeeze to a pinch. "Remind me to get you some clamps. Crocodile clips, I think." He gave a hollow huff of a laugh. "Just be glad you're facing me and not the street and all your nice neighbors when you ride my cock…this time. Now sit."

When Elliot, too startled by Drew's words and too mindful of the stretch of his ass, didn't comply, Drew tsked, brought his hands to Elliot's shoulders—and pushed him down until he bottomed out. Elliot howled at the rub of Drew's thick cock against his already overstimulated prostate. He closed his eyes tightly and bright white starbursts danced behind the lids.

"No. Eyes on me," Drew ordered and pinged them open. "Breathe with me."

Elliot tried and within a second the pain was bearable. Within two, it was shooting ecstasy through him.

"Yeah." Drew could read his body. Or face. Or maybe his eyes. Elliot didn't know and couldn't think, not poised like this, hovering on the brink of pleasure and pain and wanting both and so hot and tight he was about to shatter. "Yeah. Now ride me."

Drew helped him rise and sink, Elliot gasping as Drew's cock dragged over each centimeter of his passage. He tried to keep his head forward to look Drew in the eye, as ordered, but it lolled back, and his eyes rolled.

"I wonder how many of your neighbors can see you," Drew whispered, his voice broken. "How many are watching nice respectable antiques trader Elliot Douglas riding my cock. Maybe I should turn you round, let them see you properly, let you see them."

He wouldn't. No one was watching. But the thought, the idea… Elliot dripped with sweat from his hair down and had to fight to keep his grip on Drew's shoulders. Each rub over his prostate was pure agony now.

With an "I can't last…" Drew fucked him with several hard thrusts that forced tears from Elliot's eyes and had him clenching his teeth to keep in his screams. Moments later, Drew pulled Elliot to him and came with a low, guttural groan against his shoulder, his mouth hot on Elliot's skin and his teeth pressing into his flesh.

Startled, Elliot threw his arms around Drew and held him, his ass contracting around each heated spurt Drew jetted within him. Elliot felt each one despite the condom and he thought how he'd love to take Drew's load bare, really feel it in his ass like he had down his throat and on his face. Elliot ached from head to toe, every muscle screaming and his ass on fire, holding Drew in his arms, feeling his panting breaths and experiencing the tremors shuddering though him.

I did this. I gave him this release. Just like he did me. Now Elliot felt proud.

They sat there until Drew's breathing slowed. He peeled his head from Elliot's sweaty skin with a *pop* that made them both laugh and cocked it to one side to look at Elliot. "That was fucking amazing," Drew rasped. "Amazing fucking. Both. But you'd better move."

He really should—Drew was going soft inside him. Elliot climbed off, each limb shaky, and Drew held the base of the condom.

"Got strength to shower?" Drew asked.

Elliot shook his head. "I don't want to." Would Drew register that this was out of his comfort zone for Elliot? He'd muttered about wanting to shower after sex the last time Drew had stayed over. He'd also mumbled that their previous time, in Drew's hotel room, had been the first occasion he'd had sex without bathing after—it hadn't been opportune. He'd been too exhausted after their second session, so that made two, but now he was *choosing* not to. Another step out from behind his self-imposed walls.

Drew cupped his face in one hand and stroked with his thumb, his soft touch an acknowledgment of Elliot's words, Elliot felt. He was floating, hazy, barely aware of Drew helping him to bed and cleaning him down.

"Your face…" Drew traced the smile that must have been curving Elliot's lips. "You're gonna be sore in the morning when the endorphins fade." He chuckled. "As am I."

* * * *

Elliot was. He needed a soak in a tub, he thought, but agreed with Drew that they needed breakfast more. He hadn't expected them to be making it together.

"Sorry!" he gasped, turning from the fridge with the milk and almost spilling it on Drew when he bumped into him. "Wasn't expecting you there."

"Hm." Drew took stock of the space and where everything—appliances, cupboards and supplies—was. "How about I go there, and I do this..."

Within a few seconds, their operation was streamlined, Elliot pouring the boiling water into the teapot and the milk into the jug, and Drew slicing bread. When the slices popped from the toaster, he buttered them and passed them along to Elliot, who took up the jelly to spread on them.

"Don't suppose you're English enough to have Marmite?" Drew queried.

"I don't know what that is," Elliot confessed.

An old song came on the radio, and Drew laughed. "'You like the movies, and I like TV,'" he sang.

Elliot barely remembered the lyrics. "I take two steps forward...?"

"I'll take two steps back." Drew did a dance-shuffle, making Elliot laugh in turn.

"Things in common, there just ain't a one," he couldn't resist singing along.

"But when we get together, we have nothin' but fun," Drew capped, tempting him with a triangle of toast.

"You know it ain't fiction, just a natural fact," Elliot started, his mouth half-full.

"We come together 'cause opposites attract," Drew finished, popping the rest of the toast into his mouth.

Elliot had to sink down into a kitchen chair, he was laughing so much. He poured the tea and added milk, and Drew's exclamation had him turning, to see Drew had discovered a box of sugar cubes.

"Stand back," Drew ordered, seconds before throwing in two cubes from where he stood a few feet away from the cups. "What? It's the British version of basketball!"

'"I like it neat, and he makes a mess,'" Elliot quoted ruefully.

'"You take it easy, and I get obsessed,'" Drew added.

"Talking of, what were you saying, about handing the case over?" Elliot thought it as good an opening as any.

Drew nodded around his bite of toast. "I realized I can't take things any further alone. All I found out yesterday was that Kislyak's allegedly involved in racketeering here, but the guy who told me wouldn't talk on the record, so proving that..." He shrugged. "Oh and Kislyak just allegedly 'acquired' a hardcore BDSM club here in town in the same way as he 'acquired' a lot of his other businesses. Which would be a good angle to start an investigation with."

"Can you prove that?" Elliot asked, his heart thudding and his brain ticking over. "That he now owns this club?"

"I don't see how." Drew took a drink of tea. "That's an even more closed world than the one of art and antiques and... What? That expression on your face..."

Wordlessly, Elliot held out the invitation he'd received a few days ago, from the fetish club that had been Caress and was now, the jarring black and neon red invite said, relaunched under new ownership as Kiss. *Kiss of the whip*...was a slogan the place was using, and it all seemed very extreme to Elliot.

"Kiss— *Kislyak?*" Drew exclaimed. "You think this is the place?"

Elliot nodded. "I do. And if he's grabbed this asset off someone, cheated them, threatened them, or something, wouldn't there be talk at the inauguration? Or gossip about who he cheated, so you'd know a name to interview? Even if you didn't interview them yourself, you'd have something to solid to pass on as well as the recovered paintings."

"I…" Drew stared into space for a second, seeming to ponder. To consider. He flicked the edge of the invitation. "I'm not a member."

"Really?" Elliot's heart banged and he felt as though he'd jumped into the deep end of a swimming pool—because he refused to paddle in the baby end, wearing water wings—when he replied, "I am."

It took him over half an hour to convince Drew, especially when he laid out the preparations they could make.

"I'm still not happy about this." Drew tapped the table. "And you were *really* planning on going anyway?"

"Yes." Elliot hid his face behind his refilled cup. "You know I'm working on stepping outside of my comfort zone. *You* know that better than anyone." He was not only pushy—he could push guilt too.

"We both have to be very careful." Drew took the cup from Elliot's hand to stare him in the face. "And stick to what gets worked out and agreed on?"

"Of course." Elliot nodded…knowing he'd do whatever it took for Drew to succeed and close this case, which would then give them both a chance at the relationship they'd started…

Chapter Nineteen

"'Bigger. Bolder. Brasher.'" Elliot read the text flashing on the screens inside the club's reception. The words popping up in lurid color slashed through the moodily lit space that was almost as dark as the late evening outside. "'More exciting'." He'd been thinking the first three adjectives could be applied to him in his self-imposed quest to liven up his existence, but he wasn't so sure about the last one.

Now that he was here, *more terrified* was perhaps more accurate. The longer he had to spend on the formalities of transferring his membership to Kiss—the new version of the old club Caress—and trying to read the regulations and codes of confidentiality and conduct on an electronic tablet *and* sign in a guest, the more his courage and resolve evaporated.

"We can leave," Drew muttered, looking at him. "We don't have to do this."

Elliot heard that as *you don't have to do this* and shook his head. He *was* doing this. The first time he'd been to the previous incarnation of the club, he'd only ventured into the main room, and had sat himself immediately down at the first grouping of seats he'd seen that had had a vacant place. But the people sitting and standing there had been friendly, welcoming a newbie.

Anton, a guy Elliot had been relieved to see was even older than him—he'd been feeling ancient in the midst of all the lithe twentysomethings fluttering about—had got his sub, Tyler, to fetch Elliot a drink. The pair had been very open and relaxed in chatting about the whole Dom–sub lifestyle.

Karl, sitting with him, and who Elliot had met at the same time, had asked his sub, Lars, to show Elliot around. This had led to the next step forward Elliot had taken, that of seeking out Karl's pro-Dom services. *And that seems to have led, somehow, to this.*

"If it makes any difference, let me repeat what I said—you look so fucking hot," Drew told him.

"I feel hot." In the literal sense of the word—Elliot had never worn leather pants before. "Although parts of me are cool..." And hadn't even known there were leather pants with holes cut out there. *And there. One on each cheek.* He took a quick glance at himself in the reception station's mirror, mainly to check all was in order.

His white silk shirt, a flouncier style than he would ever have chosen, left to himself, was unbuttoned enough to show a flash of the nipple jewelry he wore. Again, Elliot hadn't known there was screw-on nipple jewelry, for non-pierced nubs...but he did now.

He still wasn't sure what the silver circles with their four screws that finished in fat round heads represented. A ship's wheel? Compass points? What he did know was that the jewelry pinched, making him gasp when a twinge caught him unawares, and that the silver balls hanging off the bottom screw were heavy. He was glad about the masquerade masks club users were invited to wear, especially that he and Drew had chosen ones that were bigger than mere domino eye masks. Elliot's was pale, denoting his sub status, while Drew's was black.

"This is modern," Elliot observed, turning his wrist for the assistant dealing with their paperwork to attach the wristband. He was used to ones whose color showed what a wearer was there for, but these had an electronic cell to register when its wearer had reached the two-drink limit.

"Doesn't apply to non-alcoholic drinks, of course." Their facilitator winked, which seemed fitting for his shiny red latex devil costume, one that had the shortest shorts Elliot had seen in a long time. Drew had asked him a few casual-sounding questions about the new management, but gotten only vague, marketing-spiel-type answers.

"Make sure to hydrate." The red devil handed them a small bottle of water each to show what he meant. "Now, go get some Kiss!"

"Wonder if that should be go get some at Kiss," Drew muttered as they walked through the door that a huge guy in leather bike garb—including the requisite booty shorts—opened for them.

Elliot took a minute to steady himself. The club's large open socialization space was now darker and edgier than it had been when the place was called Caress, with louder, more pulsing music and flashes of light. Even the couches, chairs and tables in their little groupings looked more modern designs. It wasn't exactly the makeover he would have given the place.

There seemed to be more subs on leashes than there had been the few times Elliot had been before, and he didn't recall the costumes being so extreme. He frowned, trying to puzzle out the harness equipment that two burly men were holding out in front of a tinier blond guy, who was shaking his head and pressing his back against the wall. He understood when the sub was forced to his knees, then all fours, for his Doms to fit the saddle and bridle to him.

The blond's protests stopped when the metal bar of the bit filled his mouth. He was led away by the leather reins and spurred on by the leather crop thwacking across his ass before Elliot could see how he was reacting. Did he still seem reluctant? Was that an act? Whatever, this new atmosphere seemed more heavily charged, harder-edged, and it was a club in which Elliot looked demure compared to some.

The loud slap and a high-pitched cry, followed by the cheers and whoops of the people gathered around, suggested at least one spanking bench in an alcove was in use already. "One," came the count, in a half-dozen voices.

"Make the next one hurt the toppy little bitch," ordered someone in a low, guttural command.

"Try the bar? See if we can get talking to people? There's a good few gathering there," Drew suggested, walking ahead, with Elliot following as they'd arranged. *"Bloody hell."*

Elliot, reaching the short counter, understood why it was popular spot. He tried not to stare at the servers, but it was hard not to when their animal hoods with ears invited spectators to guess what they were dressed as, with the furry pouches holding their cocks and balls providing more clues…all of which could be confirmed by the type of tails curving from their butt plugs. The four graceful, athletic-looking young men seemed to do a lot of bending over and jiggling about, making the tails swish.

"I'd say 'I bet they get a lot of tips' but it sounds like a bad pun," Drew muttered.

"This place used to be more charming," Elliot said.

Drew laughed. "Only you would call a fetish club charming. Oh."

He stiffened and checked that his mask was covering his face. Elliot turned to see where he was looking. A man strode through the main room of the club, a small group of people at his heels. He was masked, the dark color showing he was a Dom, as if that weren't obvious by the dominant air he gave off.

There was more than that to the man. Drew conveyed a sense of control, or authority, too, but his was effortless, part of him, whereas this man, surveying his surroundings and the club's users arrogantly, wielded power as though he enjoyed using it for its own sake. *Or for cruelty's sake.*

That he was wealthy was obvious from his clothes and accessories and the way he expected people to do his bidding. Those with him weren't friends but an entourage, his acolytes, Elliot surmised. The man's presence changed the club's atmosphere a little more, and not for the better.

He didn't need to ask but murmured, "That's him, I take it? Kislyak?"

Drew nodded, staring at the small group.

"Fine." The old Elliot would never have come into contact with a person like that, someone who was gripping a young sub's chin and examining him as if he were merchandise. The new Elliot didn't intend to be here, wearing this painful nipple jewelry, any longer than he had to. He took in the deepest, longest breath he could, letting it fire him. He was here and he had a goal he'd set himself. "Let's go get this done."

Before Drew could stop him, he'd hurried through the club's patrons and reached the small group of men. "Mr. Kislyak?" he said, wriggling through the man's followers.

The man turned, his mask blacker and more extreme than any Elliot had seen so far but his eyes were darker still. He looked Elliot up and down, and it felt like small insects skittering over him.

With difficulty, Elliot held in a gulp. "Could I talk to you, in private?"

His entourage laughed, some even gasping, but Kislyak silenced them with a raised hand.

He tilted his head back so he looked down at Elliot. "Maybe…because it so happens I'm looking for a new sub. But I always try before I buy."

Before Elliot could answer, Kislyak let go of the young guy he'd been examining and reached for Elliot instead. His meaty hand shoved Elliot's shirt off one shoulder, ripping the fabric a little, then fondled a nipple, pinching the nub that was already squeezed by the silver ring. Elliot cried out in surprise and pain.

"That's a good start." Kislyak's lip curled in a sneer. "What else you got to offer? Anything worth my time?"

The man's European accent, something Elliot hadn't expected, threw him. As he stood there, confused, Kislyak tsked and turned to go. "Wait." Elliot stepped into his space. "I'm an art dealer. A broker." He slipped back into the moneyed drawl his father and uncle and everyone he'd been at prep school with spoke in. "I have clients in the Middle East who are after certain artists for their palaces. They have a wish list, you might say."

"So go to a fucking auction in London or New York and get them some." Kislyak wasn't as tall as Drew but the way he stood with his head back to look down his nose made him seem it.

"It's not as black and white as that." Elliot swallowed. "They're not prepared to wait until artists they seek come up at auction. They'd rather be more proactive than that."

The film of sweat dewing most of his body wasn't to do with the heat in the club or his leather pants. He and Drew had mentioned him using this cover story should he get into conversation with anyone who looked like they might have information on Kislyak, and here he was trotting it out to the man himself. He could feel Drew lurking behind the group of people surrounding them. *How long before he rushes forward and stops this?*

"Hmm. You might just be worth talking to. Let's take a walk." Kislyak threw a heavy arm over Elliot's shoulders. "Just us two," he ordered his coterie. "We're taking a tour." And that heavy arm bore Elliot away.

Shit! Drew stared after them, his skin crawling at the sight of that bastard with an arm around Elliot. This wasn't good. They hadn't planned this, much less discussed it. Kislyak wasn't anyone's fool. *Damn Elliot! What the hell does he think he's doing?*

His heart thudding, Drew sprang forward after Elliot—right as the lights and music changed and the guys from behind the bar rushed into the space where Elliot had been, whooping and shrieking, to start their floor show. A crowd gathered within seconds, surrounding the dancers, whistling and cheering their gyrations, and following them when they trooped off in a chorus line to parade around the open space and arrive back at the bar, on which they climbed and struck poses.

Drew didn't care about that. All his concern was for Elliot, who was nowhere in sight, but was presumably still with Kislyak. He wanted Elliot away from him and right now. They'd had to leave their cell phones at reception, so there was no way to call Elliot and get him to leave. Drew doubted he would, anyway. Elliot seemed to have a lot to prove.

His lips thinning, Drew just hoped that Elliot managed to press the switch on the pendant dangling from his nipple shield, which held the recording device. Drew slipped the earpiece from where it was tucked inside the collar of his military-looking frock-coat-style shirt and jammed it in his ear. *Yes!*

"Like the improvements?" Kislyak was asking.

Drew still couldn't see them. Were there private rooms here?

"Know what it all is?"

"I think so." Elliot didn't sound too sure. "The spanking benches and St. Andrew's crosses in the main room, yes of course. Did I see power points for electro play in those alcoves just before we come this way? Oh, and that's a restraint bench?"

Footsteps suggested they were on the move.

"And a sex sling?" Elliot continued. It sounded as if it were in use.

"And a fisting sling," Kislyak replied, his voice gleeful. "I love fisting. Gonna be quite the show later. And in here's the med fet suite. Should be some punishment play in here soon." He sounded pleased to hear it.

"You own this place?" Elliot asked.

Kislyak must have nodded, because there was no reply. Drew hoped he was going the right way after them. Power points and padded benches—the alcove Elliot had mentioned! A man was testing a wand and the buzzing fuzzed up the electronics Drew was listening through. *Fuck.* He slipped through a gap in the wall and found himself in a short corridor which held the private rooms Elliot and Kislyak had just been describing, overseen by staff monitoring.

A door marked 'Private' served as an invitation to Drew and, casting a glance behind him, he went in, and the door clicked behind him. The room didn't hold much beyond a console with two huge monitors, both of which were divided into several smaller squares, each showing an area of the club. He'd found the control room, where security monitored images sent from the surveillance cameras…one of which showed Elliot and Kislyak in what looked like a small office.

Kislyak was sliding a drink across the desk to Elliot and pouring himself one from a bottle of vodka. The hairs on the back of Drew's neck rose, whether at that, or the pair being alone, or the hidden-away, basement feel of the room.

"Now." Kislyak turned to Elliot. "You gonna cut the bullshit and tell me why you're really sniffing around me? Because that art broker story? Was fucking laughable." He slammed the bottle down on the desk with a loud bang that made Elliot jump…and made Kislyak laugh.

Chapter Twenty

"*Shit, shit, shit.*" The wire Elliot was wearing was transmitting not just to Drew but to the party Elliot had spoken to, and hopefully to his team back in London. Well, at least Claire, after he'd been in touch with her earlier and emailed her a copy of his case notes. She'd been alarmed and a little horrified at how rogue he'd gone but had promised to fill in the rest of the unit, including their superiors…if she could make them listen.

Drew also hoped that, not being suspended, she was in a stronger position to involve local law enforcement should that be necessary. Was it? Elliot had made his own arrangements, paralleling Drew's, but again, Drew had no idea if the backup they perhaps needed was there.

Breathing out through his nose—something he remembered from a managing stress workshop, although he couldn't recall what it did—he stroked Elliot's face on the monitor, willing him to get the hell out of there.

Instead, Elliot took a sip of his drink. "Of course it was. Oh, by the way, I actually do have an antiques shop here in town, you know. But yes, I wanted to get a chance to meet with you. You're a hard man to get a sit-down with."

Kislyak grunted. "I'm sitting now." He even took off his mask, a short nod telling Elliot to do the same. Again the barely restrained violence of his movements struck Drew.

"I'm a lawyer." Elliot removed his mask, although the fact he was donning another wasn't lost on Drew. Drew's mouth fell open as Elliot described what he could do for Kislyak, or more precisely his businesses, particularly his international ones, once Elliot had set up a chain of companies, one controlling the other, to facilitate management of Kislyak's enterprise, mainly its cash-flow and tax burden.

"Look me up," Elliot invited his host. "You'll see my family law firm has been successful at this for many years. Elliot & Elliot."

Kislyak looked up from his phone after a few seconds with a laugh. "They lost their licenses to practice law."

"But *I* didn't," Elliot replied. He let that settle for a couple of seconds. "I 'wasn't involved' in the business." He made air quotes to go along with his denial. "But I am in the new one we're setting up now after paying the fine and lying low. We can help with creating as many 'companies' as it takes to move money around and we have contacts with several banks." He took another sip of his vodka and set the glass down.

Drew could hardly bear to listen to all this. It wasn't just the deception, although he knew how Elliot felt about that—but the improvising, with Drew stuck in reactive mode, not knowing which turn the conversation and events would take. Jesus, was this how that Claire, or his team, felt when he went out on his own like this? If Elliot's heart was thumping and crashing as hard as Drew's was at this, Drew would be able to hear it on the feed.

"You have a lot of business in the state," Elliot prompted.

"It's a big state," Kislyak countered. "And I have a lot of business everywhere."

"Exactly."

Elliot was losing focus now. *Get out of there!* Drew commanded him. His hands clenched into fists.

"Well, I've made my case for how I can help you avoid taxes and launder money." Elliot stood. "So I'll leave it there for now."

Kislyak stood too. "You don't go until I say. We have a lot more to discuss."

"We do?" Elliot asked. "Like…?"

"You're a sub." Kislyak came around the desk. "And I'm a Dom who's into punishment. Oh, not 'funishment'. His expression showed his contempt of that. "I enjoy enforcing punishments the sub doesn't like. I like pain play that tests a sub's limits."

"I don't… I'm n-not…" Elliot stammered.

"I don't care. What I do care about is some stupid crusading detective thinking he can touch me!"

That was it. The end. The fear on Elliot's face, fear he was trying to hide, had Drew racing to the door to get to him—and finding it locked. *The hell?* That click when he'd closed the door had been it locking? He wrenched at the handle, not caring if he alerted the security personnel…who should have been in here watching the monitors…

Ice-cold trickles of fear sliding down his nape to his spine, he spun back to the screen that showed Elliot. Brave Elliot, forcing himself out of his safety zone…into the unknown. *Stupid Elliot!*

"You think I don't know who's snooping around after me?" Kislyak yelled. "You think I didn't set all of this up, control it?"

Drew whirled around to kick at the door, but it was solid. He missed Kislyak's next words but caught the name *Silver*. So Kislyak had left a trail, gotten Drew here…into a trap. No, not just Drew—*Elliot*.

"I'm coming, babe. Hang on," Drew promised him through teeth he was clenching so hard he was surprised they didn't grind into nothing, searching along the console for an override to the door-locking mechanism.

"*I* don't send a stand-in to do my dirty work," Kislyak said, looking right into the camera in his office…right into Drew's eyes. "Hello, DS Andrew Harrington. I want you to back off, stop looking into certain areas of my life."

"How you pay experts to plan heists and steal from museums for you," threw in Elliot, despite the obvious fear that had him gripping the edge of the desk.

"Pay— I *am* the expert, you fucking pile of crap!" Kisylak roared. "That's my legacy, and I'll reveal it when I'm ready."

"You just revealed it, you moron!" Drew yelled back at the monitor.

Kislyak pulled in a breath, calming himself. "But maybe this will convince you to back off." He leaned away and must have opened a desk drawer, because he straightened, with a pair of thick, heavy-looking leather gloves in his hand. He donned one and the light in the room gleamed on the item's reinforced steel knuckles, an addition that made the glove into a knuckle duster. The second glove was different. Black leather, like the first, this was covered in evil-looking metal spikes, studding the back and along each finger and thumb.

Now Elliot darted for the door to find it locked, and pull and kick at it, as Drew had done to his, to as little avail.

Kislyak laughed, the cackle pulsing with evil and menace. "This is my place! Think anyone's gonna come in? Particularly when I'm disciplining a sub? You have no idea how much I'm going to enjoy this, fucking you up and knowing Harrington's watching and unable to save you." He pulled the gloves on tightly.

"Red. *Red!* I do not consent! I do not give my consent to this act!" Elliot yelled.

Two things happened at once. Elliot screamed, high-pitched and anguished, and the monitor feed cut off, leaving Drew, his blood pounding in his head, staring at a blank screen.

Drew lost it. He threw himself at the door, ramming his full weight against it again and again until it started to give. The door was solid and breaking it down hurt, but Drew felt no pain, only fear for Elliot and anger at himself for letting this happen. He'd learned his lesson—he'd stepped away from the case, but his previous obsession had cost him dear. *Cost me Elliot? No. Please God, no.*

With a final crack, the door's hinges gave enough for Drew to boot it open. He powered through, barreling into someone outside, a tall guy who grabbed for him.

"Wait—" the man tried to say, but Drew wasn't inclined to. The guy should have been glad that all

Drew had time for was to deliver a punch then shove him over when the impact had the guy staggering.

Drew bolted for the main floor of the club and into a chaos of panicking bodies, screams and shouts, bright lights and water spraying down from the ceiling sprinklers. A low siren noise started, confusing the people milling around even more, as did Drew when he pushed them out of his way in his desperate race for the short corridor off the alcove behind the bar. The office where Elliot was imprisoned had to be there.

"Out of the way!" Drew raged at a group of men blocking the space between the bar and his destination. "Move, you fuckers or—"

"Whoa." A middle-aged black guy in the doorway was right in his face, stopping him, signaling to another to pin his arms behind his back. "Andrew Harrington? I'm Frank Heise, FBI." He flicked his ID in Drew's face. "A friend of Elliot," he added, when Drew still struggled.

"FBI?" Elliot's friend? The guy Elliot had worked with to blow the whistle on his family and who he'd called in on this. Even so, Drew couldn't spare the time to deal with that now. "Elliot screamed—"

"That was the signal, yes." Frank indicated his team. "Can we let you loose?"

Drew nodded, but still couldn't take any of it in, not when he'd yet to see Elliot. As soon as he was released, he pushed through the small knot of people in the office—to Elliot. "Elliot—!" was all he could get out. He raced to him and grabbed him in his arms. "Elliot, you're okay?" he demanded, clutching him tightly and feeling the nod Elliot, holding on to him in turn, gave in reply.

"That bastard didn't lay a finger on you? Where is he?"

"Arrested," someone—Frank, Drew thought—replied. At least two officers were speaking at the same time, about Kislyak having been under suspicion, the value of the recording Elliot had obtained and the leverage this and the arrest gave to the investigation and—

"Pity," Drew spat. He'd have liked a few minutes with the bastard, the case be damned. He held Elliot's head to his chest, Elliot's head shakes and his shudders taking Drew's whole body along for the ride.

"Get a blanket—anything, to cover him up!" Drew yelled, not wanting anyone to see Elliot like this. He snatched at the jacket that was offered and wrapped Elliot in it, tilting his face up to see for himself that he was okay.

"He didn't touch me," Elliot told him. "Frank's team got here."

Drew noted the phrasing. So the team hadn't been here earlier? Elliot hadn't given him the signal that he'd seen them, so maybe they hadn't been in place, and Elliot had gone ahead with this anyway, putting himself in such danger? "Why did you go off on your own like that?" Drew demanded, his heartbeat still galloping. He glared at Elliot. "To teach me a lesson?"

"*What?* No!" Elliot pulled free and scowled in turn. "To help you, you idiot! To solve this! To—"

"How about not doing this here, either of you?" Frank butted in, glaring at Drew too. "Why don't you take him home and give him the care he needs, and you, Elliot, let him?"

Elliot sagged, and Drew caught him. Frank was right. Nothing else mattered, not even details of the case against Kislyak, either here or in London, or which branches of the Met or Drew's superior officers there were involved and where Drew now stood.

He held Elliot hard to him the whole ride home and even once they were inside Elliot's house and in the bathroom. Drew only slackened his hold to undress them both and turn on the shower. As soon as the water was hot enough, he stepped in, bringing Elliot with him. Eventually, under the warm spray, with Drew mindlessly rubbing the washcloth up and down his back, Elliot stirred.

"You're washing me?" he asked as if he'd just realized.

"I'm taking care of you," Drew corrected. It did feel like administering aftercare, following a scene. "After which, we're burning your club membership and those leather pants."

Elliot laughed. "Don't you like me in them?"

"I like you better out of them." Drew looked him up and down. "Come on. Let's get you dry and into bed…where I can really take care of you."

And he did, starting by gently licking and sucking on Elliot's still pink and still swollen nipple. It was bare of the silver shield and Drew supposed the FBI had taken it, for the recording device concealed in the pendant hanging from it. He hoped Elliot had removed it himself and not let any of the officers get their hands on him. He didn't neglect the other and had Elliot purring and under him—Drew hadn't realized how sensitive his nipples were. Which was when he blew on the wetness he'd left and made Elliot writhe.

Elliot squirmed when Drew sucked his balls, feeling them fill and harden on his tongue, then thrashed when Drew took him deep. The slow, almost languid pace

Drew set had Elliot sighing, but he groaned when Drew used the tight wet heat of his mouth to bring Elliot right to the edge…then pulled off. The noise became a moan when Drew used his hand to jack him, instead, equally as slowly, catching Elliot's sighs and gasps in his mouth as he kissed him the whole way through it, even when he rubbed his thumb over the head of his cock.

"Drew!" Elliot cried out when Drew stopped again. "Drew!" he moaned, when Drew switched his hand for his mouth once more and flattened his tongue, taking Elliot to the back of his throat.

He loved the way Elliot's breathing and pulse sped, his release threatening. Drew rubbing the tip of his thumb on the bundle of nerves just below the head of Elliot's dick had him rocking his hips, then thrusting them, then his cock throbbing as he came hard down Drew's throat. Drew swallowed every drop, licking Elliot clean after.

"Ohhh." Elliot gave a sigh of perfect contentment but wasn't too dazed or sated to take Drew in his hand and stroke him off. "Don't clean me," he whispered after, almost too tired to speak but helping Drew milk out the last drops. "Like wearing you…"

Drew lay on his back and tucked Elliot's head under his chin, falling asleep holding Elliot clasped tight. They had a lot to sort out, both from the case they were involved in and because of what lay between them. He smiled to find his thoughts and hopes running on not the former, but the latter. On him and Elliot. He could only hope that the next day brought positive developments…in all areas.

At least he had plans on how to start the day well.

Chapter Twenty-One

Elliot loved the blow job Drew woke him up with the next morning and how natural it felt for him to slip down the bed himself, so they were sixty-nining, both licking and sucking the other, and learning what brought their partner to a shuddering, sighing release. The shower after was a lot more fun than last night's, then he and Drew had one of 'their' breakfasts, as Elliot thought of them.

As before, they meshed together, this time with Elliot catching the toast as it shot up from the toaster and buttering it for Drew to add a layer of spread to it—cherry jelly for Elliot, and Marmite for Drew. Elliot still wasn't sure what that black stuff was, but he'd buy a jar every week if Drew pinned him against the counter and kissed him like that for it, his tongue probing and dominating…and sharing the smoky, spicy taste of his preferred breakfast food with Elliot.

Elliot had the memory of that kiss to keep him going when they parted after. A discreet team of FBI officers, including Frank, came to speak to Elliot and take his statement, while Drew was shut away with his laptop, undergoing a series of interviews with several different parties.

"Hey." Frank nudged Elliot as he and his team went to leave. "It'll be okay, you know. You and..." He jerked his head to the room where Drew was working. "Just trust, okay? Whatever happens, you'll handle it."

Whatever happens... That was just it. Elliot had no idea what was coming next. His life was here, and Drew's in London, where he'd for sure be taken off suspension and probably given his own task force to head up, to finish the investigation into Kislyak. Or would that be pursued from the States, now? Well, Drew would be the UK branch of it. *UK branch.* Elliot mocked himself and his wrongheaded thinking. *He's in the Metropolitan Police, not a law firm!*

He couldn't stop running through scenarios. Meeting Drew had changed Elliot's life and Elliot—no doubt stupidly—had dared to dream of himself as no longer alone. Facing that loneliness again after having tasted companionship and indulging in dreams of having someone of his own was a much bleaker, heavier prospect than it had been before.

The thought that Drew had crashed through Elliot's life only to leave had Elliot wanting to reach for his calendar and appointment book, reinstituting and straightening that neat, safe, parceled-out way he'd dealt with the world. Before he knew exactly what he was doing, his cell phone was in his hand and he was calling Karl. He had an appointment for tomorrow and...canceled it, leaving a message to say he didn't want Karl's services any longer, but hoped they could still meet. He disconnected the call with trembling, sweaty fingers, but felt good.

Because even if Drew had to go, Elliot couldn't go back to shutting himself off. Whatever changes were coming, Elliot promised himself he'd honor the progress he'd made, the steps he'd taken out from behind the wall. He wouldn't backslide. And whatever was happening between him and Drew, he'd meet it with dignity.

He took a few minutes' respite outside, stroking Quince, the big ginger cat from a few houses down who liked to lounge on Elliot's property. The porch really needed furniture, but nothing like rattan that the cat would scratch. Unless something like a scratching post could be incorporated into the theme and the cat trained to use that? That could be Elliot's next project. That would give him something to work at and—

"Elliot?" Drew looked a little surprised to find him out on the porch. He stretched his back and rolled his shoulders as he walked up to Elliot. "What are you doing out here?"

"I'm thinking about getting a cat," Elliot replied, not knowing he was going to say that until the words came out of his mouth.

"Really?" Drew scratched Quince under the chin then turned his attention to Elliot. "You're not a dog person?"

"I'm…not sure." Elliot didn't think that was something he'd ever considered.

Drew looked him up and down, his gaze warming Elliot where it landed. "You okay?" Drew scoffed at himself. "Yeah, dumb question after yesterday. Look, can we talk? Maybe inside?"

Elliot nodded and led Drew into the small room he'd been working in. Elliot hadn't considered having a home office—this room would have been a parlor, originally—but it would be possible to have a study-type room as old-fashioned as his office at the store, of course.

"Elliot." Drew took his hand. "I have to go back to the UK. I'm not sure for long how, not at this stage—"

"Of course." All the things Drew must have to do… He took a deep breath. "I'm nervous about flying but I'll look into getting medication or maybe hypnotherapy. I wouldn't be able to visit for a while, with all the arrangements I'll have to make, but you'll be busy too, for the foreseeable, you said. So by then we'll know which weekends we'll be where, won't we?"

"What?"

Elliot raised his eyes to see Drew looking bewildered.

"Elliot, I don't want you in pieces, or you to have just pieces of me." Drew cupped Elliot's face. "I love you, you idiot!"

"Oh. *Oh.*" Elliot raised a hand to hold Drew's face too. "You never said!" he exclaimed.

"Neither did you!" Drew retorted. He blew out a breath. "Let's start again. I'm Detective Sergeant Andrew Harrington of the London Metropolitan Police Service's Specialist Organized and Economic Crime Directorate Arts and Antiques Division and after a short relationship—very short, seeing as we started it properly yesterday—I've fallen in love with you. Your bravery, your resilience, your humor, your likes and dislikes, your looks, your ass and how you're the perfect sub to my Dom… I love all of you."

"And I love you too." Elliot took the simpler way out, adding a snarky grin that he knew he'd pay for. *Hoped* he pay for.

"And I promise to care for you, support you…and challenge you," Drew continued, a smirk blossoming on his face too.

"Oh." Elliot considered. "I…promise to always be a challenge?" It seemed his answer, which came from the heart, was the right one by the way Drew pulled him into his embrace and kissed him. Thoroughly. At great length. He touched his lips when Drew let him go and wondered if he had stars in his eyes.

"They were hinting I'd be offered promotion." Drew patted his laptop to make his meaning clear—his bosses back home. "So I wondered how you'd feel about a permanent move to London?"

"I…I don't know." Elliot blinked. "It's…"

"Very soon," Drew finished for him. "And I like it here, which is why I wanted to explore other options." He sat on the edge of the antique table, something that would have given the old Elliot palpitations. Now, Elliot sat beside him, his hand in Drew's, listening.

"I've been obsessed with work and proving myself—whatever that means—for as long as I can remember, and I've learned it's wrong, that there has to be a balance. No, that I have to *make* a balance."

Elliot nodded. He'd come to understand that too.

"But I'm a detective. I don't think I couldn't be," Drew went on. "But I can consider a change…" He grinned. "Did you know that the Texas Police and Sheriffs have a fledgling Art Theft Detail, and would welcome a Scotland Yard consultant to share insights for their training programs and seminars, for instance?"

Elliot shook his head.

"And your friends in the FBI have been telling me about their Art Crime Team, which deals with art and cultural property crime cases. Seems the Washington HQ would like more links with the UK, and the unit here in the south-central region looks interesting. And then there's Interpol. I work with them already—"

"Really?" Elliot hadn't known that.

"Only slightly, but they'd be happy for me to take a more weighty role within their cultural heritage crimes program." He pulled Elliot close. "But you know what? I think I'll take a sabbatical while I decide. What do you think?" He kissed Elliot, stroking his tongue deep.

"Mmm." Released, Elliot wondered if he looked as dazed as he felt. "I think...you should take as long as you like." He kissed Drew back, maybe more hesitantly, but exploring in his own way. Drew loved him! *And I love him.* The future stretched itself out before them, their life together, as a unit, filled with challenges... Which reminded him. "I do have one question. What sort of dog?"

* * * *

Six months later

Elliot had never been inside the Devereaux Hotel before, either prior to or since its refurbishment, so should have been more interested in the remodeling and décor but took nothing in, and not because he was more interested in the food and drink at this Friends of San Antonio Museums gala dinner and auction.

He was interested in their friends, seated at their table, of course, enjoying seeing Aldric, Darrell and Jonas dressed up, along with Trent, their latest Intrinsic Value staff member, a student from the Heights, where Jonas was teaching. Meredith, glamorous in an evening gown, was also at their table with her beau, and Jim Devlin, the interior designer, beamed from his seat next to his Bexar Bear Stephan, a big and hairy, mild-mannered pediatric nurse.

He should have been paying attention to the speech currently being given, because this was about Drew's work, the Bexar County Museum Security Group he'd put together, but he couldn't really take much in, not when Drew, seated at his side, had his hand on Elliot's upper thigh…and was moving it upward.

"The sharing of intelligence on security issues between public and private sector organizations within the sector reduces crime across the sector," the chairman of something announced from the podium, to applause.

Elliot gasped, not startled by the man's words, but by Drew rubbing his crotch. Drew was looking at the podium and nodding, yet his warm and firm hand was cupping, *there*, and getting Elliot hard in a second.

"Safeguarding visitors, collections and cultural heritage means keeping up to date with important security alerts as they happen," the speaker informed them, to more general agreement from the audience.

Drew chose that moment to undo Elliot's zip.

"I…" Elliot clutched the edge of the table, crumpling the cloth. Drew paused. "…couldn't agree more," Elliot finished. They'd discussed his exhibitionist tendencies, and Drew helped him to act on them. *Forced* him to act on them, via scenes that had ranged from fucking Elliot while he kneeled, naked, on the wide ledge at the uncurtained bedroom window to having him give Drew head on the patio in the back garden. And now this…

This was Drew's fingers inching inside Elliot's fly and seeking him out while their friends were seated innocently around them.

"Sharing intelligence from cultural venues across the county with our members—who are not only museums but galleries, archives, libraries, historic houses and archaeological sites—in this way enables us to identify emerging threats and adjust our security responses appropriately!" the chairman thundered.

Elliot hoped the applause covered the moan he couldn't hold in when Drew rubbed his thumb over the head of his cock in slow, firm circles and the squeak he emitted when Drew dragged his thumbnail into Elliot's slit. Drew took his hand away so he could use both to clap and although Elliot felt cold, he was relieved. His dick pulsing, he'd been leaking pre-cum and was moments from spurting.

But any relief he might have felt was short-lived—Drew brought his thumb to his lips and licked it, making eye contact with Elliot as he tasted his essence. Checking no one was watching them, he sucked his digit into his mouth, sucking and tonguing at it, and Elliot felt the swipes of Drew's tongue and the pull of his lips on his cock that was now poking free of his pants.

"Elliot, no zipping up until I say so," Drew ordered, his voice too low for anyone else to hear, but sending prickles down Elliot's spine.

"What? Why?" Elliot started to ask, but the forefinger Drew held to his lips in a gesture for silence stopped him. Drew pointed toward the podium—

"To Detective Sergeant Andrew Harrington from Scotland Yard's Arts and Antiques Division, a big thank-you!" finished the chairman, beckoning.

"You heard me?" Drew checked with Elliot before standing and making his way to the platform.

The gala's guests stood and applauded as he headed to the top of the ballroom, their table clapping and cheering the loudest.

"Elliot?" Aldric looked puzzled. "Aren't you going to stand and honor Drew with us?"

"I'm..." *Paying tribute to his expertise in my own way,* Elliot thought, and hoped he didn't say it out loud.

Chapter Twenty-Two

Drew was well aware of Elliot's struggles and also knew something that Elliot didn't—that they weren't over yet. He'd allowed Elliot to do his fly up before they'd left the table, hiding his smirk at how carefully Elliot was forced to do this, and at his subsequent attempts to hide his erection.

"Yeah, the Interpol job will involve some stays at the headquarters in Lyon, France, and some at the UK base in Manchester," he explained to Jim as they circulated before the charity auction. He was excited about his new role in countering trafficking in cultural property, a big part of which would be analyzing emerging trends in art thefts. "Elliot's looking forward to traveling with me."

"And Aldric to managing the store in my absence," Elliot added.

It would mean more hours at Intrinsic Value for Trent, the new assistant Elliot had taken on, something Drew wasn't sure the guy would want or need. Trent didn't seem the type to be working in an antiques store to make ends meet, and wasn't he on a sports scholarship anyway? *None of my business, any more than Jonas' relationship with the guy is,* Drew told himself.

He nudged Elliot. "Let's go sneak a look at the new room Jim mentioned?" and was soon sweeping Elliot away into the not-yet-opened orangery or palm court or whatever the hotel was calling it. Whatever the name of the venue, it looked like a conservatory to Drew, and a pretty one at that, with the moonlight filtering in and stars visible through the domed roof. He made sure Elliot saw him lock the door behind them, closing off access from the hotel.

The room's far wall was glass, a bank of French windows, in fact, looking out onto the street...also meaning that people could look in. Drew had tested visibility earlier, peering hard through the panes to find that they were still covered in frosted-glass spray paint. He'd checked with a room attendant that this was the case and had been assured it was, with the new space not being ready for its grand unveiling quite yet. Drew doubted Elliot knew this though.

"What I did earlier, getting you aroused when you couldn't come..." Drew started.

"Yes?" Elliot's careful tone and expression said he understood that Drew had brought him here to this secluded nook for reasons connected to that, but he wasn't exactly sure which.

"Come here." Drew led him to the court's fountain, proud in its center. It was splashing, albeit faintly, the mechanism running to test it, and a wide waist-high rim ran around the basin, keeping the water inside. It would also serve as a seat for Elliot, once Drew let him sit on it.

"You didn't think I'd leave you like that, did you?" Drew asked, and dropped to his knees on the circular base below.

Elliot had time for one quick, nervous glance at the floor-to-ceiling windows, but then Drew had his pants undone and shoved down, along with his boxer-briefs. He eased Elliot down to sit, and Elliot squeaked when his bare ass made contact with the stone. The shock didn't diminish his arousal—he was erect in Drew's hand in seconds.

With a "And you claim to be so modest," Drew grabbed the base of Elliot's cock and sucked the head into his mouth, coating his tongue.

Elliot jerked, so Drew held him tighter, cupping his balls too. "I know. All those windows… Anyone could look in and see you getting your dick sucked," he commented. "And you're going to sit there and take it."

Elliot gasped but didn't pull away. Drew licked Elliot's slit, scooping out pre-cum and squeezing Elliot's balls harder. "Gonna swallow you down," he warned, taking Elliot's dick to the back of his throat. Elliot had come to love being deep-throated and had on one memorable occasion fucked Drew's face as powerfully as Drew liked to fuck his.

"D-Drew…" Elliot hiccupped, fisting his hands in Drew's hair.

"Thrust," Drew instructed from around Elliot's cock and Elliot did, driving his dick hard into Drew's mouth.

Drew sucked as Elliot pumped. Like this he couldn't use his tongue tip to trace the vein that pulsed the length of Elliot's dick, only rub the flat of his tongue over it. He knew he was massaging the bundle of nerves on the underside of the crown when Elliot shouted his name. Evilly, Drew slid his fingers beyond

Elliot's balls to stroke the soft skin behind them, then slipped farther back to circle Elliot's hole…before pulling free of Elliot's cock.

Elliot whined, his hips thrusting and his breath catching.

"Oh, you thought this was gonna be a quick blow job?" Drew asked. "Over in a few seconds? Oh no—there's not much risk of being seen at that. Or if anyone saw, you could just pull out and zip up, no problem. No. Let's see how you manage when I'm balls-deep in your ass, right here, right now…just like you need."

"*What?*" Elliot whipped his head from side to side, searching into every corner of the room and beyond, outside.

"Didn't you wonder why we haven't fucked in a few days?" Drew asked. He'd done it deliberately, wanting Elliot craving his cock. "You're *desperate* for me."

He watched the struggle of emotions play out on Elliot's face, and how Elliot followed Drew's movements when he ripped open a sachet of lube and slicked up his fingers. "And as we don't use condoms, you'll be going back into that fancy gala full of me," he murmured.

"Dripping with you," Elliot whispered, his eyes enormous.

"Sit on the edge and lean back," Drew instructed, yanking Elliot's boxers and pants down farther. He waited for Elliot to comply, exposing his hole then stroked around once before pushing in. He was so attuned to Elliot's reactions that it was like experiencing Elliot's pleasure with him, starting with the throb of the nerve endings in the tight ring of muscles as Drew penetrated them.

"Oh, so *tight*," Drew breathed. "I see your stripes." The last spanking Elliot had taken had been with the cane, and Drew smirked now, remembering Elliot shifting and squirming in his seat the day after, when they'd been in the brasserie for lunch. The red welts were still visible.

Drew unzipped himself with his other hand, but doubted Elliot noticed, not when Drew, still stretching him, grazed his prostate. He liked the jump and gasp Elliot gave, so did it again, making. Elliot's hole clench and ripple around his fingers

"*Drew!*" Elliot pleaded.

"Yeah." Drew relented. "I have to be inside you, feel you around my dick." He slid free and lubed his cock with the rest of the slick, then lined up with Elliot's ass. He grabbed Elliot's ankles and brought his legs to rest on his shoulders.

"Eyes on me," he ordered, wanting to watch Elliot's irises darken as Drew entered him. "Love this moment, when I penetrate you." He pushed in as slowly as he could stand, forcing his swollen cock into Drew's tighter-than-usual opening. "Tell me how it feels."

"Pleasure," Elliot gasped, his body undulating. "And scary. Anyone could—ah—see…"

"But you need it." Drew growled and thrust his hips, almost unseating him from his perch on the edge of the fountain…and penetrating him to the hilt. "That's it. Take it, babe," he gritted out, willing himself not to come at the first tight clutch of Elliot's channel, but ease back and forth in long, deep strokes. He'd ordered Elliot to keep his eyes on him, but Drew couldn't resist looking where he was almost all the way out, leaving only the broad head of his cock inside Elliot to stretch his hole around it.

"Drew, I need to come." Elliot's voice was a reedy thread.

"I know." He would have taken care of Elliot himself if he didn't have to keep a hard grip on his hips. "Get yourself off."

Elliot's weight and balance shifted when he loosened one hand from where it held the stone ledge to fist his straining dick. The sight of him working his red, leaking flesh and the sound of the wet meaty slaps made Drew thrust harder and faster, fucking Elliot with his thick shaft over and over.

"*Drew*!" Elliot shouted as he came, and the mingled need and ecstasy in his voice and the way he bore down on Drew's shaft made Drew swell inside him, as he came, his release fierce and hot, spurting high into Elliot. Coming in his ass as Elliot jetted over his hand and—*oh, God*—his suit was indescribable. Drew rode the wave, feeling every muscle cramp with the blinding, deafening white heat of his climax.

He gave one last thrust, just because he could, and pulled free, mainly as he had to lower Elliot's legs from his shoulders. The series of tight little noises Elliot probably didn't know he was making stroked Drew's soul. He dropped Elliot's feet to the fountain's base and kneeled on it again, holding him through the last of the tremors still shivering through him. *Through me too.* He'd never come as hard as he did with Elliot.

When Elliot stopped quivering, Drew stretched up to kiss him, the fierceness of possession softening under Elliot's acceptance and love. *Love. "I love you,"* Drew mouthed against Elliot's lips.

"*Love you too,*" Elliot mouthed back.

He helped Drew up to sit beside him on the fountain's ledge, and them, there, in the starlit glass-walled room was perfect. Drew grinned.

"What?" Elliot asked, suspicion lacing his tone.

"Oh, just thinking…that the next step is The Box," Drew replied.

"The new BDSM club?" Elliot looked confused.

The private, carefully vetted members-only was due to open soon in the city and they both suspected Karl was a part-owner. Drew nodded. "Yes. You know that huge St. Andrew's cross, on the platform in the middle? Well, I know you do—I saw you eyeing it when we looked around the place. Eyeing it and fantasizing about being on there, taking a whipping from your Dom…and any Dom he might choose to loan you to. Well, I've arranged…"

He bent close to whisper the rest of what they'd be doing on the equipment in full view of the club patrons on opening night, and Elliot's eyes popped at the same time as his breathing seized. The shy yet wicked smile that curved his lips was the most perfect sight Drew had ever seen, just as Elliot was the most perfect partner he could ever want, and their life together the biggest challenge either of them could ever imagine.

Want to see more from this author? Here's a taster for you to enjoy!

Hooked on You: In Deep

Bailey Bradford

Excerpt

"Come on, kids, let's see if we can find any shells!" Titus Eisenhower nodded to the parent volunteers forming a human wall between the Pre-K children and the ocean, keeping the kids from getting in past their ankles. The annual field trip to the beach was one of the highlights of the school year for the kids and teachers alike.

Seeing the children's faces lit up with joy, hearing their shrieks of—mostly—laughter, watching them run and splash in the bit of water they could reach…it made his heart swell every single time he got to take part in this trip, and this was his fifth with one of his classes.

The other teachers were at his sides, vigilant—when it came to children and water, all parents, all *adults*, needed to be watching the whole group.

This year's parents were great. He'd only had one pissed-off dad who had refused to let his child go since he couldn't just hang out with his kid. Other than that, there'd been plenty of parent volunteers, and, wonder of wonders, they were all pretty awesome, too. Last year, two of the dads had gotten into a fist fight over some perceived insult. *That* had been a disaster.

"God, I bet we don't ever get such a great group of parents again," said Stacy Evans, his best friend and colleague. She'd been hired the same year he had, and they'd become fast friends. Stacy's bright-orange hair was all over the place as the beach breeze whipped it about. She shoved uselessly at several flapping strands. "Why, oh why don't hair ties work for me?"

"Honey, that hair can't be tamed any more than you can," quipped Michelle Ochoa. She was older than Titus and Stacy, but not by too many years. "You're as wild and powerful as the wind."

Michelle was also Stacy's girlfriend, though no one but Titus knew that.

Stacy laughed. "Whatever. When I'm blinded by my own hair, then what'll I do?"

"Mr. Eisenhowew, I finded a shell!" Little Bobby Garza hopped in place as he waved a sandy glob in the air. "Wook!"

Titus grinned and jogged over to Bobby before squatting so he could be eye to eye with the boy. "Hey, you did! That's awesome! Want to dip it in the next wave and see if we can get the sand off?"

"Yes!" Bobby's delighted shriek made Titus' ears ache, but the rest of him filled with sheer wonder and delight. He loved his job, and he loved the kids, loved seeing them grow and learn. It made him less cynical every time he saw shining wonder in a child's eyes.

"Then let's do it."

Titus got the other kids to show their treasures. A couple were upset that they didn't find *good* shells, but, overall, everything was going surprisingly well.

After they got the kids lined up—and allowed the parent volunteers to take their kids home in their own vehicles, rather than making them ride the buses—Titus took a moment to look back at the ocean. The waves were slight, which was normal for this area of the coast. It was only one-thirty in the afternoon, so the sun was high and bright, the reflection on the water exquisite in its beauty.

"Just think...next weekend, we're going to be here in our own beachfront condo, partying—or relaxing, more likely—for a whole seven days," Stacy said, her soft voice breaking into Titus' quiet appreciation of the view.

Not that he minded. He grinned at Stacy. "You and me and some margaritas," he promised.

Stacy nodded. "Darn right. I'm so looking forward to it."

"Me, too." Titus and Stacy had started their beach tradition their first year at the school. Michelle and Stacy hadn't been dating then. They'd fallen for each other a little over two years ago, but Michelle didn't come to the beach vacations. She had prior commitments with her family in Michigan that took her away.

Titus privately thought Michelle didn't want to intrude, and he had mixed feelings about that. He didn't want to be a third wheel, but he hated to think Stacy might regret Michelle not being there.

"Stop brooding," Stacy said, poking his arm. "You're going to get wrinkles all over your forehead and around your eyes before you hit thirty if you keep doing that."

"I wasn't brooding," Titus protested, immediately trying to smooth out his features.

"Yeah? Then what were you frowning at?" Stacy asked.

"Y'all need to hurry up—we have to get on the road," Michelle called out to them.

"Oops, we're holding everyone up." Titus grinned, relieved at being saved from having to answer Stacy's question.

"I'll keep bugging you until you answer me," Stacy promised as they rushed to the buses.

Titus could have protested, but he knew better. Besides, all he had to do was tell Stacy the truth—he didn't want her to feel like Michelle wasn't welcome.

But he'd keep the other truth to himself—that he was lonely, and when he'd looked out over the water, that sense of loneliness had permeated his happiness, and now, melancholy lingered in the place where joy had been. Yes, he'd definitely keep that secret.

PRIDE
PUBLISHING

About the Author

A native Texan, Bailey spends her days spinning stories around in her head, which has contributed to more than one incident of tripping over her own feet. Evenings are reserved for pounding away at the keyboard, as are early morning hours. Sleep? Doesn't happen much. Writing is too much fun, and there are too many characters bouncing about, tapping on Bailey's brain demanding to be let out.

Caffeine and chocolate are permanent fixtures in Bailey's office and are never far from hand at any given time. Removing either of those necessities from Bailey's presence can result in what is known as A Very, Very Scary Bailey and is not advised under any circumstances.

Bailey loves to hear from readers. You can find her contact information, website details and author profile page at https://www.pride-publishing.com

www.ingramcontent.com/pod-product-compliance
Lightning Source LLC
LaVergne TN
LVHW041925090826
845145LV00015B/739

* 9 7 8 1 8 3 9 4 3 7 3 3 5 *